PENGUIN METRO READS

ISHQIYAPA

Once upon a time in a sleepy town called Chaibasa, in Jharkhand, there was a boy very, very unhappy with his name—Pankaj Dubey. It seemed like his parents had named him only out of a sense of duty without giving it any proper thought. However, unlike his ordinary name, he wanted to do extraordinary things! He once gifted a basket of lemons bought from Mangla Haat to his first girlfriend's mother to impress her. The mother made 'achaar' out of it but her daughter changed her 'vichaar' about him. Hence, he went through the most lemony break-up! He spent most of his growing-up years aping breakdance steps of Mithun in *Disco Dancer*. Because he spent so much time with his hero, Aryabhattaji blessed him with a zero in his maths paper.

Pankaj Dubey travelled to Delhi and Europe for his higher studies. Between living in a dingy flat in Mukherjee Nagar, New Delhi, with four IAS aspirants, and becoming a paying guest of a toilet cleaner in Coventry, England, he thinks he has seen it all. He once forgot to switch off his mobile phone as a broadcaster with the BBC World Service, Hindi, in London. To his distinction is the contribution of making all serious listeners of BBC News hear the popular tune of the movie *Saathiya*: 'Saathiya, maddham maddham teri geeli hansi'.

While in college, he filled the North Campus of Delhi University with laughter. Pankaj was awarded the Navodit Lekhak Award by the Hindi Academy (Government of Delhi) for penning down creative ways to waste time during one's college life in the campus, in his story called 'Mukhauta'. His humour expedition continued in the Coventry University in West Midlands, England, where he did his master's in applied communications.

A babe-sitter by passion and babysitter by compulsion, he is presently based in Mumbai and experimenting with screenwriting in the Indian film industry. This book is also a part of such explorations.

For more details visit www.pankajdubey.com
Facebook: /carryonpd
Twitter: @carryonpd
E-mail: carryonpd@gmail.com

Also by the same author

What a Loser!

ISHQiYAPA

PANKAJ DUBEY

Penguin
metro reads

An imprint of Penguin Random House

PENGUIN METRO READS

USA | Canada | UK | Ireland | Australia
New Zealand | India | South Africa | China | Singapore

Penguin Metro Reads is part of the Penguin Random House group of companies
whose addresses can be found at global.penguinrandomhouse.com

Published by Penguin Random House India Pvt. Ltd
4th Floor, Capital Tower 1, MG Road,
Gurugram 122 002, Haryana, India

First published in Penguin Metro Reads by Penguin Books India 2015

ISBN 9780143424512

Typeset in Adobe Caslon Pro by Manipal Digital Systems, Manipal

Printed at Repro India Limited

www.penguin.co.in

PROLOGUE

'Babu . . . I want to devour you,' she said.

This was Sweety. Her lips were painted magenta-red. She had a thing for magentas. It was that dangerous bloody thing between dark pink and dark red.

Sweety was actually going through an intermediary state of life. But for the moment, she wanted to deface his chest.

She held him in her slim sandalwood-infused arms. Her arms reeked of the Mysore Sandal soap she used daily to keep the aroma alive. He loved that smell, but today it was suffocating him. He wanted to push her away, even as she reached out to unbutton his shirt.

'Are you afraid or what?' She eyed him suspiciously.

'Come on.' He gathered himself and tried to kiss her on her eyes.

She did not want such sweet innocent shots of love. She was ready for a torrential downpour of raging hormonal romance.

'Let me kiss you all over on your chest. Let the world know . . . Babu is *my* property,' Sweety said breathlessly as she clasped his wrists and tried to unbutton his shirt.

He lightly shoved her, straddled her and unzipped his trousers. His boxers were pristine-white with a red jockey band.

'Your underwear has changed . . . *You* have bloody changed. Babu, you hiding something from me, aren't you?' Sweety let out a muffled protest.

He gagged her with his thick parched lips. They were cold like dried wax. He interlocked his sweaty palms with hers. She could sense the tension in every drop of the sweat coming off his palms.

It was time to take matters into her hands literally!

She had him on his back, as she pushed against him like a tidal wave. Sweety was now on top.

The flashy light from the bulbs bordering the huge mirror of the vanity van fell straight on his face. His skin had sheen, quite like the moonlight. Sweety kissed him all over his face, bent down over his neck and got down to unbuttoning his shirt. He held her hands off like a cuff.

'Why won't you let me unbutton your shirt? You are behaving very strangely, Babu, what has happened to you?' Sweety was sure that something was up.

Sweety's hand held his shirt and was desperately trying to unbutton him.

'Just a sprain. I was at the gym . . . uh . . .' He uttered some lame words.

'You know what . . . when you look right . . . you are lying,' Sweety attacked him straight.

'You know what! You over-read. Don't look at me like that . . . I just had a sprain. That's it.' He tried to push her away.

'I can't make love to my Babu? Do I need permission now?' Sweety asked petulantly.

She was overtly sexy. Her sex appeal was attached even to her pretty little chin; it was that soft conical chin, which became sexier as she pouted to show that she was upset.

'Come on, love me . . . pull off my jeans,' he said. Whether it was a request or an authoritative instruction, he wasn't sure. In fact, he was not sure about anything at that moment.

Sweety kept staring at him.

'Go down,' he whispered. 'Pull off my jeans, Sweety.' His voice trembled.

Sweety looked deep into his eyes. His eyes were light brown. In the guide book of coital flirting, dating a guy with light-brown eyes is the riskiest! Sweety did everything that was 'risky' for sure!

She scrambled down. He eased a little. He let go of her wrists. He adjusted his head on the little cushion of the vanity van. He knew that Sweety was about to give him waves of pleasure. Sweety unzipped him. He simply surrendered. Like a predatory cheetah, Sweety changed her course. In a matter of seconds, she tore his shirt. She knew something lay hidden beneath that shirt.

She was shocked. And speechless.

He was hiding something for sure.

There was a tattoo on his chest. It was the name of a girl. And it wasn't Sweety. It was 'Anu'.

The tattoo looked fresh. The skin around it was still red.

There was another woman in his life. Sweety could sense that she had been taken for a ride.

She punched his nose. A punch on the nose can shake your whole body—it is bloody hurtful. She left him wounded and bleeding. He owed her an explanation but she was not in a state to listen to one.

'Sweety—' he tried explaining but she was beyond it.

Sweety was high-strung by nature and would swing between extremes. She felt extreme love for him. Or may be extreme hatred for him—both emotions tearing through her at that very moment. There were no in-betweens here.

Some young girls and boys standing outside the vanity van could sense that some steamy lovemaking was definitely underway inside the mood-lit and cosy vanity van. The door of the van suddenly opened with a bang. All the heads turned towards the door. They saw a man's shoe being flung like a missile and then another. Nobody could miss the vanity bag that came flying next. All the crew members waiting outside were witness to the most dramatic scene that was not even part of the shoot.

Sweety walked out of the vanity van with her magenta lipstick smudged around her lips. She stormed out as if she was playing her part in an epic war saga. Nobody knew her on the set, at least none of the people standing around the vanity van. Her walk was super confident, reminding them of Chulbul Pandey from *Dabangg*. This filmy swagger was all but a ruse to keep people guessing whether she was a heartbroken girl or simply a catty bitch who broke the noses of handsome men. It was not easy to get to know the bundle of contradictions that Sweety Pandey was.

Two different worlds had been shaken, right to their core!

But things had not been this way 112 days earlier.

112 days earlier . . .

1

'How dare you chain Ashutosh?' She slapped him on his left cheek. The right cheek was already swollen and red. This resounding slap by Sweety kind of balanced the colour contrast on his face. Now both his cheeks were equally red.

He was meek—meeker than a mouse that scurries into a rathole whenever it sensed danger. He was the meekest and the newest servant at her command. He was yet to go through 'Sweety's Crash Course' on living and surviving in the bungalow.

'Sweety baby, he's dangerous,' replied the half pigeon, half mouse of a servant.

'Ravi, Suraj, Srikant, Ashwin, Somesh, Nitin, Ashutosh!' Sweety called out.

A violent and fiery brigade comprising a variety of breeds came jumping and licked her all over lovingly.

Sweety lived with these seven samples of canine supremacy. She loved to adopt dogs and name them after guys she had broken up with. Sweety was thus surrounded by Dobermanns, Alsatians, greyhounds, German shepherds or even Dalmatians— all the breeds there were to have.

Sweety had dumped seven guys while she was still in school. She actually believed that men were dogs. Sweety was the one who chose her men and dumped them on the lamest of pretexts. Sweety's bungalow flaunted these dogs. Her plush bungalow was a colour riot. There was nothing natural about the place. Each wall vied to be the brightest of them all. Even tube lights and fans reeked of the black money that financed them. None of the ceiling fans were simple white ones; all of them had some unique Mughal-style embellishment, too gaudy and garish to be part of a twenty-first-century home. The bungalow looked like an overdone, showy set of Hindi films in the 1980s where even the dining table with all the surrounding chairs was made of white marble. It even had an old style revolving mirror-panelled bar!

Kaali Pandey, Sweety's father thought of himself as no less than an emperor. A five-time minister from Motihari in Bihar, he lived in Patna, the city of power-hungry eagles.

Kaali Pandey was unapologetic about his demeanour which was no less than that of a mighty demon. After all, he had been the kidnapping mafia kingpin for two decades now. He was involved in the biggest kidnapping cases and his name spelt fear. Businessmen, doctors, engineers, all dreaded his name. They started moving their kids out of Bihar to keep them away from becoming Kaali Pandey's targets. It was a time when the mafia ruled the badlands of Bihar—a time when crime was at its most organized form in the state. The educated and the law-abiding were terrified by the criminalization of politics and the politicization of crime in the state. The state was inhabited only by those who wanted to rule or were ruled out of no choice.

One fine day, Kaali had a change of heart and decided to use his might and power to contest the assembly elections. The most notorious criminal went on to become a minister. Even fate fell in line when it came to Kaali Pandey.

Kaali's energy and genes were transferred to his only daughter, Sweety. She was the lonely lioness of this family. Kaali's wife had died when Sweety was only three.

A motherless daughter is like an unfettered tidal wave. She can be torrid enough to bruise the skin of your feet at times or can sweep you off your feet by gently caressing your heels. Sweety was actually another extreme—uncajoled, uncaressed and uncuddled.

'From today, if any of you chain my boys, you will be chained in return!' announced Sweety.

'I will take care,' a scared servant apologized.

'You'd better.' She sounded like a dictator—the result of the genes of a ruthless mafia king and politician.

Scoffing in anger, Sweety went inside her room. Sweety's bedroom would put a Barbie dollhouse to shame. It was a reflection of the little squirrel sitting inside the lonely lioness's heart that was Sweety's. The room had been done up by her friend Saumya who had just enrolled in an interior designing course in Delhi. The room was enveloped in all shades of lavender: lilac-pink and lavender-purple walls, bed, net, dressing table, curtains, shower curtains and whatnot. But Sweety never thought of herself as Cinderella or the tiny Thumbelina. She did away with all possible tenderness a woman needs to possess to secure a place in a fairy tale.

Saumya was her best friend. She had allowed her to use her fairy-tale imagination to decorate the room. She often asked her not to try and make her soft.

'Saumi . . . don't make me a *janaani* like you,' Sweety often reminded Saumya.

She somehow hated and yet loved the fact that Saumya brought out the little woman in her. Right from helping to choose the right cup size of Sweety's first bra to putting together an elaborate and highly secretive method for the disposal of sanitary napkins, Saumi had always mothered the carefree Sweety. Sadly for Sweety, Saumya had left for her course three months earlier. That was the main reason for her disturbed state.

But Sweety had always lived the life she wanted to. She did what she should have done at her age. She had boyfriends, she dated, and she dumped them. She learnt to play the guitar from a cute-looking home tutor and had also learnt by heart Britney Spears' lyrics from YouTube. From her home in Patna, she fantasized about living in Paris.

This list was too cool to be true for a Patna girl. But Sweety had done it all!

Kaali Pandey gave her everything she desired but would not give her the freedom to leave Patna.

Sweety raged at the fact that she was being caged in the house when her best friend went to Delhi to live on her own. She knew that Kaali would fulfil all her wishes but not this one. Saumya was her only window to the world outside. Sweety wanted to go to the US to learn music and wanted to be a pop diva someday, but her father made sure she never even got her passport.

Sweety rested her head on the head board. She took a deep breath and closed her eyes. She slipped out her mobile phone from the lavender flip studded with hearts made of crystal. She scrolled through the names in the phone book and stopped at a name coded with asterisks and hash signs. She looked at the number uncertainly. Her fingers played a nervous little game of chess deciding whether to call him or not. There are numbers on our phonebooks which tempt us to call them. We debate with ourselves; at times, we pick up the courage to call the number and at times we just let it be.

Sweety was not the sort to let it be. She knew what she wanted. She called the number. It went unanswered. She called the number again.

A man's voice whispered, 'Sweety.'

Sweety turned cold and numb, as if she had been struck by thunder. She cut the call and pressed the button for the phone to shut down for as long as she could.

2

26, Boring Road, Patna
Kaali Pandey's *baithak*

Though the entire mansion was an excuse in the name of style and class, the owner of the house made this personal space ever so more dramatic that it still stood amidst all the unnecessary baubles and multiple hues.

Kaali Pandey's baithak was audacious and lurid. Kaali Pandey was sitting on his maroon sofa with a deer skin spread on the back rest. Though hunting is punishable, Kaali never hesitated to boast about his lawlessness. He owned and displayed skin of various carnivores and protected species such as tigers, leopards and lions.

He was the *dabangg*-est minister from Motihari. Once a kidnapping-mafia kingpin, today he was the minister of the public works department. His cavalcade of goons had been replaced by a cavalcade of security guards. His henchmen were all but a thing of the past but his own style and flamboyance had never changed.

Kaali retained only one character from his past, a man who had been his special security person for three decades. His name was Ghonchu. Ghonchu actually means a dumb person. Such men are picked and trained to be more faithful than dogs. Ghonchu was named so because of his slow mental functions. Kaali Pandey mobilized him and made him his right hand.

Ghonchu was all muscle and girth in the wrong places. He had a crooked body structure, right from his jaws to his feet. It made him look like a zombie ready to fire his desi *katta* with his beedi-stained mouth. Kaali Pandey would trust this crooked-looking crook with his life.

That balmy summer morning, Kaali Pandey was in his drawing room under Ghonchu's protective eye. A private deal was being struck between Kaali Pandey and a Gujarati businessman, Mukesh Patel. Some heated negotiations were on.

'I extracted a ransom of ten lakh rupees, almost thirty years back, when the market rate was as low as just a lakh,' bragged Kaali Pandey, his gold-plated tooth glittering boldly.

'I am from Gujarat, bhai saheb. I don't know a thing about Bihar. It was a terrible idea to start a business here. My son just got married, bhai saheb . . . and he's been kidnapped here. Please get him back,' pleaded the Surat-based businessman. 'Five crores is what they have demanded! I am a Gujju, but that doesn't mean I have a diamond mine. Arrey, bhai saheb, my cloth business was in shambles. Otherwise why would we have traded in Bihar?'

'You took dowry worth three crores for your son. Add two crores more and the ransom is ready!' Kaali Pandey offered.

Kaali outsmarted everyone when it came to negotiating money.

'Bhai saheb . . . you are a PWD minister. You have so much power, so much might. If you don't help me, who will? I have always funded your party.' Mukesh Patel's safari jacket was bursting at its seams. His man boobs were visible through the grey safari suit which looked a decade old and it almost seemed as if the worried Gujarati had a cleavage. Men with breasts give a clear signal—they are loaded. Kaali Pandey knew it well.

'Okay, I'll save your son. You give me my saving commission of two crores . . . you earn three crores profit plus the life of your son,' announced Kaali Pandey without a shadow of shame on his face.

Mukesh Patel looked too confused to be relieved.

'No worries. Go arrange for the money. Your son will be back,' Kaali comforted him.

Ghonchu gestured at Patel to touch Kaali Pandey's feet. Mukesh did as he was told.

The blissful assurance was followed by an awkward moment of silence which was shattered by a loud thud. Someone had attacked the low hanging chandelier. It hung precariously half-broken.

It was Sweety.

This was the seventeenth chandelier to have become the victim of Sweety's temper.

Kaali Pandey found his untamed princess standing fearlessly, unapologetically in front of him.

He gestured for the audience to vanish. Ghonchu started purposefully leading Mukesh Patel, who was gaping open-mouthed at Sweety, away from the scene.

Father and daughter stood in front of each other—face-to-face.

'When will I get my passport?' Sweety was curt.

'You don't need a passport,' replied Kaali Pandey in his most sombre tone.

'I feel like I'm in a jail,' Sweety barked.

'I have given you enough freedom.'

'These dogs and I are no different . . . We are in chains!' growled Sweety.

'Don't start that again. You are not chained—' Kaali was trying to purr like a cat.

'I want to go see the world.' Sweety was in no mood to negotiate.

'The world is in our hearts,' Kaali tried to throw in some philosophy.

'Don't fool me. I am eighteen, not eight!' Sweety retorted.

'You are not going out of Patna! Anything else?' Kaali stated the final word.

'Driving . . . At least let me learn to drive,' Sweety dealt her secret card.

'I don't want any tamasha,' Kaali rejected.

'Then be ready for a bigger tamasha!'

'Ghonchu will teach you,' Kaali simmered, his voice low.

'You want me to die? Driving school . . . I have few numbers.' Sweety flaunted a list, letting Kaali know of her intentions.

'Call Lallan. He will teach her driving,' Kaali instructed Ghonchu and left the room.

She was Sweety. She was unstoppable.

3

The jaded Maruti 800, brick-red in colour geared up to glide from Kaali Pandey's magnificent marble-arched porch. 'Lallan Driving School' was pasted on the glass of the back door. It had scratches and scribbles and the red paint had come off in places and had been fixed by nail paint. The car was in a semi-disposable stage with dents all over the body.

Out stepped Lallan, a handsome, six-foot tall, young man with his shirt half tucked in, his hair half set, half ruffled and a smile that looked half natural, half plastered. Everything about him was half-baked—his dressing sense and mannerism. Lallan looked at the mansion like a guide who is so used to seeing the Taj Mahal that there is no excitement left. Suddenly feeling a bit conscious, he retrieved a small pocket comb and tried to put his hair into some semblance of order and bent to check his reflection in the rear-view mirror of the car with a furtive glance. He straightened up as he could see a girl peeping out of the French windows, looking straight at him. It was the same silhouette he had seen many times earlier; but he had never dared to return the look. He could figure out that he was being watched and cold fear crept into him all over again, like it had on all past occasions.

No stranger to this place, Lallan stepped inside the bungalow. The dogs barked at him zealously. Lallan looked at one particular dog. It looked more ferocious than the rest. It was an Alsatian—light brown, with sharp canines, tearing on a mutton bone. A mousy male servant was handling the dog.

'New one?' asked Lallan.

Before the servant could nod his head, he heard a big burp. Minister Kaali Pandey had just finished his breakfast of hot jalebis and crispy pooris. He had also guzzled lassi which had dyed his slick, black moustache into something that resembled a shiny-white toothbrush. He was sitting at the dining table, looking like a monster.

'You duffer, you try to run away from me, huh?' roared Kaali, looking at Lallan.

'I was busy finishing my MBA. My exams are still on . . . I have two papers left,' said Lallan.

'You should have joined my force officially. What will you do with this degree?' Kaali mocked.

'Business,' Lallan immediately reacted.

'Ambani, come . . . sit down.' Kaali's mockery annoyed him. Lallan clenched his fists.

'Amitabh Bachchan . . . Angry young man . . . Why did you not smuggle my arms to Purnia?' questioned Kaali.

'I am not doing illegal stuff any more. Please don't force me.' Lallan had come ready with an explanation.

'Tata . . . come, come. Sit down. I have a job for you,' Kaali got up from the table and wiped his hand with a tissue and threw it at Lallan. Lallan ducked.

Suddenly Sweety came down the spiral staircase. Kaali could see that his daughter was watching Lallan. Then father and daughter looked at each other in the eye. Neither one blinked. Lallan realized that Minister Kaali Pandey was now looking at someone standing behind him. He turned around.

Lallan and Sweety were now face-to-face.

'He will teach me driving?' Sweety scanned him from head to toe.

'Yes,' Kaali announced.

'Doesn't look like he knows his job well.' Sweety's scrutiny made Lallan uncomfortable.

'He knows it! I trust him and his family!' Kaali barked at Sweety.

Sweety walked towards Lallan. They were now inches apart. Lallan had earlier seen only silhouettes of Sweety. For the first time, he could see her big black eyes; he could see a beauty spot on her left cheek; he could see a cleft on her chin; he could see a temperamental beauty standing in front of him. He stared wide-eyed for the longest time ever. He couldn't make out if she was beautiful or he was too caught in the moment. Whatever it was, he was hooked.

'Tomorrow at four in the morning,' ordered Kaali.

'I sleep late nights . . . Studying for my papers.' Lallan's voice became humbler.

'If you fail in your papers, you can attempt again. But if you fail at Kaali's work, you won't get a chance again! Am I right?' Kaali's audacity was beyond question. He could be authoritative at any moment in his life as if he was born with a certificate to rule over people.

Lallan went mum. He had had a strange relation with Kaali Pandey since his early childhood. He hated him from the deepest core of his heart, resisted him, but ultimately always ended up surrendering. It had become a habit, a ritual he had been going through for years now. He questioned the thirty-seven deities whose elaborate statues adorned his temple at home but never found his answers. Lallan had given it up, totally to his fate and Kaali Pandey.

'Before the sun rises, driving lesson should be over. You come sharp at 4 a.m. Sweety learns for an hour within a radius of one kilometre. My security battalion will follow it. No one should know that Sweety is in the car or that she is learning to drive.' Lallan went blank with such complicated instructions being barked at him at breakneck speed.

'Clear?' enunciated Kaali Pandey.

'Clear.' Lallan had no option.

Lallan was now unofficially a driving tutor to the daughter of the most menacing don-turned-politician of Bihar, Mr Kaali Pandey. Kaali Pandey who was excessively possessive and guarded about his daughter and had to reluctantly give up his stubbornness and let Sweety learn to drive. It was perhaps karma that the man who was infamous for kidnapping thousands of kids for over thirty flourishing years was insecure about letting his daughter step out of the mansion.

Sweety gave a smile of triumph. Not only was the smile as wide as the Nile, but it was also as deep as the Pacific Ocean. She had beaten the forces for the time being! Sweety was pleased with herself. She had finally got the licence to step outside the cage. Every morning at four. She had always thought that she was a born lioness. Born to roam free, born to live life on her own terms.

Lallan had a dark shadow lurking around his eyes, darker than the lunar eclipse. He knew that he would always live a controlled life. He hated it with all his heart, but was there a way out? He knew the answer very well: No.

Lallan's confused eyes accidentally met Sweety's. She winked.

4

The alarm screamed its lungs out. Sweety got up with a squeak. She ran to the washroom, splashed her face with cold water, took a short cut to brushing teeth and gargled with a green mouthwash. She wiped and rubbed her face till her nose turned pink. She changed from her nighty into a pair of jeans and a grey T-shirt. Her hair resembled a cobweb; she made a loose bun and pinned it up with a Reynolds's pen. Sweety didn't even bother to check herself in the mirror.

Lallan did not have to be woken up. He was already up and cramming his Philip Kotler marketing book. He kept the book aside as his mobile let out a whistle-like alarm. He took his jacket which was hanging on the door, wore it and stepped out of his home. Lallan's mother saw her son leaving. She closed her eyes and prayed. Whispered prayers, only heard by the gods—the thirty-seven deities who resided in her temple and in her very soul. The very same deities who had not been very receptive to Lallan's long-felt existential crisis!

Sweety did not get a chance to lose her patience. Lallan was there sharp at four.

Sweety had a little torch in her hand. She flashed it on Lallan who was walking up to the veranda. Lallan stopped as the light from the torch lit up his face.

'Punctual!' exclaimed Sweety.

'We have an hour to get the first lesson,' Lallan was to the point.

Sweety smiled and moved towards the carrot-red Maruti. She opened the clumsy door and got into the driving seat. She tried to adjust the seat to her comfort.

Lallan sat beside her. He was sitting very stiffly, almost like a giraffe riding a see-saw. His discomfort was visible. His hands were shaking.

'Will you teach me or do I need to teach you?' Sweety asked him, watching his trembling hands.

'Seat belt,' instructed Lallan.

'Move,' counter-instructed Sweety.

Lallan turned the ignition on, avoiding any debate. He knew Sweety would not put on the seat belt. Putting the seat belt on would hurt her ego. After all, she was the daughter of Kaali Pandey!

'So you need to remember the basic principle of ABC starting from the right side of your feet, A for accelerator right at the right foot, B for the brake in the middle and C for the clutch which is on the extreme left. Yes, your left hand should always be on the gear.' Lallan was a real master.

'It's going right,' Sweety screamed.

'Go left,' hurried Lallan.

She took a sharp turn steering it hard. Lallan held her hands to get the grip right.

He had touched her for the first time. His heartbeat raced like the fastest sprinter who could win gold every time at the Olympics, without fail. To touch Kaali Pandey's daughter was like touching a naked wire with thousand megawatts running through it. She was hot. Perhaps the hottest surface he had ever laid his hands on, even if accidentally.

The rear-view mirror was flashing with the images of Kaali Pandey's security detail in gypsy vans. All his bodyguards were now shouldering the additional early morning duty of safeguarding this driving programme planned for his only legitimate daughter, Sweety Pandey.

The sun was still in hibernation. Only the headlights were lighting up the road around the Kaali Pandey mansion. Some street dogs were badly disturbed by this unusual drill that had started but no one was thinking about them.

Sweety smelt of sandalwood. Lallan smelt of Old Spice. The men in his family were still taking the Old Spice legacy forward.

The misty smell of sandalwood and the divine pungent smell of Old Spice swirled inside the tiny red Maruti 800.

They had started their journey—their first journey together. A journey where someone was learning and someone was earning—earning his living.

5

B.B. Gupta Institute of Management

B.B. Gupta Institute of Management, where Lallan had enrolled in the MBA programme, was the first of its kind in Patna. Though Lallan had dreams of going to the US and the UK, he was stuck with his family business.

Backed by a multibillionaire family that owned a chain of sanitary hardware stores, BBGIM had the best washrooms amongst all of Patna's private colleges. That they had the best bathroom fittings was flaunted as the USP of the institute. Washrooms were kept extra clean, as a matter of prestige. As far as cleanliness was concerned, the washrooms were the most sacred place, and the management believed that a building's dignity was measured by its cleanliness. The filthy stairs and corridors stood out in stark contrast to the washrooms.

Lallan was sitting on the wide steps of the college gallery with paan stains squirted all around him like subway graffiti. He had the Hindi edition of Philip Kotler's book in his hand. The book was the bible of young management aspirants. They end up trusting Kotler more than anybody else around them— Kotler's verdict was final. But Kotler became inherently dangerous when translated into any regional language. The increasing demand for Kotler's book had led to ambitious and often illegal editions in Bhojpuri, Maithili and Magadhi for the ease of students who were not comfortable with English. The issue of copyright never bothered the management of BBGIM as, in their scheme of things, copyright simply meant 'right to copy'.

Lallan was busy playing *kattam kutti* (tic-tac-toe) on the back of his Kotler book. He loved to play this game. It was an easy puzzle, unlike his life which seemed ready to fall apart at the drop of a hat.

A timid girl in a green-and-mustard salwar kameez came and sat down next to him. He did not acknowledge her presence. Her neckline plunged down almost to the bra line. She oozed no sensuality though—not an ounce. She lingered, brushing her bare arm against his. He flinched.

'Meetu, you know I don't like this touch-wuch thing.'

'Jhaji . . . For how long will you run from me?' She knotted the end of her dupatta around his ring finger. Lallan resisted violently. He slammed down on all her attempts to get cosy.

'I am completing my *solahwaan somwar vrat*, sixteenth Monday fast, today . . . I deserve you!' Meetu pulled him close. The term solahwaan somwar is quite a popular practice in rural north India, where girls fast for sixteen Mondays to achieve the spouse of their choice.

'I screwed up my paper . . . I will fail!' Lallan wailed.

'I will screw the one who fails you!' She almost bit him on his lips.

He looked restless in her hold.

'Don't worry. B.B. Gupta is Papa's *chela*. I will make sure you don't fail,' she tried to calm him.

'Why are you planning to waste my life?' questioned Lallan.

'Will your life be wasted if you marry me?' Meetu said, getting a little aggressive.

'You know I have other plans!'

'Yeah, I know. It's been five years now . . . You are still stuck with your bloody MBA,' she retorted.

'My dreams are big. I want to become someone . . . someone very big. Someone like . . . like . . .' he stammered.

'Like what? A grand slave?' Meetu was blunt enough.

'Meetu!' shouted Lallan, now thoroughly offended.

'You are just a slave on an EMI for Kaali Pandey! That's it. You'd better realize it.'

Lallan went silent. Meetu moved away.

'My papa is meeting your papa today. They are going to fix our marriage,' Meetu said in a tone of finality. Then she got up and left him alone on the stairs surrounded by those bloody paan stains.

Lallan felt stuck like a crow on a naked electric wire. He was a sitting duck and he had nowhere to run. There were so many reasons to feel sorry for him, but there was simply no way out.

Fear sometimes makes men crave for intimacy and other primal things.

He was surprised by his own basic instincts. Sweety smelt of sandalwood. It made him think of wild, weird things and made him feel both nervous and yet bold. He hated the smell even though it was intoxicating.

Meetu was his childhood friend. Her father was an excise inspector and a very dear friend of Lallan's father. They belonged to the same caste and had bonded over that. While the fathers bitched about people from other castes and communities, the kids played together.

Meetu had always loved Lallan. To her, he was a desi Superman. But he never did anything Superman-like for Meetu. He had never saved her; had never cared for her. He never went out of the way for her. He never gave her surprises. Nor did he ever help her in tough situations. But he was still her Superman.

Lallan, on the other hand, had never loved Meetu. He found her unattractive. He didn't find her bunny teeth cute. He thought her overgrown hair looked like a matted broom and nothing like that of the fairy-tale diva Rapunzel. He didn't find her voice sexy; he found it coarse and distorted. He felt she was too intrusive. Lallan did not like anyone who interfered in his life so much. There was already a big scar from an earlier intrusion which had left Lallan in this state of helplessness.

He just wanted to be left alone.

6

Sweety was standing under the shower. The Mysore Sandal soap slid from her arms to her slender neck and to her bosom. Her wet hair fell in place with the droplets of water trickling down.

Sweety pulled on a light-lavender robe and stepped out of the shower.

She walked to her dressing table, picked up the hairdryer and stared at herself in the mirror. She rarely looked at herself in the mirror. The music player was blaring as usual. She broke into an impromptu rendition of her favourite song. Sweety hated Hindi songs. She only loved to hum along to her favourite Britney Spears numbers.

Britney was singing, Sweety was singing, and the hairdryer was whirring. But she didn't care. Sweety had broken into a merry dance in front of the mirror. Spears's 'My loneliness is killing me' ran parallel with the dryer's dry, growling sound. Sweety secretly dreamt of becoming a pop diva. Living a cosseted life, singing to her favourite songs on YouTube became her hobby. That had been her daily ritual after returning from school. For hours and hours, Saumya and Sweety used to practise together, with Sweety singing along with a rolling tongue to get Britney's American twang just right.

'Hit me baby one more time!' She switched off the hairdryer and blew on the little curls crowning her forehead. In front of the mirror, with a pretend mike in hand, Sweety was a different person. She was a diva.

While she was engaged in her performance, there was a knock at the door. Sweety hated to be disturbed.

'I don't want to have juice today!' she announced.

'Yeah, baby . . . That's why I got beer for you,' said a familiar voice.

Sweety ran to open the door. It was Saumya.

'Saumi?!' Sweety was surprised and delighted.

'See? I haven't even gone home. I came straight to meet you from the airport.' Saumi hugged Sweety.

'I was wondering how to wait for three more months. It's difficult living without you even for a day, yaar. Ask me how I am living here? Papa will not let me go anywhere.'

Saumya flopped down on the bubble-gum-pink beanbag.

'It's okay, baba. I am there for you!' Saumya's assurance always had merit.

'You were supposed to come after three months, right?' Sweety enquired.

'Delhi is too hot. I got a small project in Varanasi. Thought I would take some time out and come to Patna for a day,' Saumi had an angelic smile on her face.

'I have my plans ready.'

'Shh! Are you mad?'

Sweety looked around.

'We will talk about all this, but not here. Later.' Saumi tried to calm Sweety down.

'But Saumi—' Sweety had so much to say.

'No, not here. I doubt everyone,' Saumi mumbled as they stepped out of the room. She glanced at Ghonchu standing in a corner, waiting for Kaali to come out of his room.

The two girls hurried down the corridor.

'Saumya!' a coarse voice called out.

Kaali had spotted her. Saumya went and touched his feet.

'Tell Guptaji that he should meet me at least once. He is always busy counting money these days,' Kaali said.

'I will tell him, uncle,' Saumya smiled. She really had an angelic smile, more mature and warmer than other girls her age.

'Papa, can I go with Saumi to her house?' Sweety implored, but her eyes were hard.

'Ghonchu, stay with her,' Kaali ordered.

Sweety looked at Saumya. Saumya smiled, cautioning her not to rise to the bait.

Saumya was the daughter of B.B. Gupta, who owned the biggest sanitary hardware chain in Patna. Gupta had never passed the eighth standard, but had always nursed a dream of holding a management degree. He opened a management institute instead. He was an old ally of Kaali Pandey, having funded him all through during the elections.

Saumya's house was the only friend's place Sweety had implicit permission to visit. Saumya and Sweety had studied together, played together, shared boyfriend stories with each other. Sweety wanted to go to Delhi with her, but Minister

Kaali wouldn't hear of it. He always wanted to keep his daughter under his supervision. He feared her getting kidnapped.

'Did you feed Ashwin?' Sweety asked Ghonchu.

'They are all overfed. You want to kill them?' Ghonchu replied. Only he had the audacity to be a little rough. His audacity was forgiven, taken for stupidity.

'Yeah, I want to. Let him die. I don't care,' she said, walking out with Saumya.

'You named your new dog Ashwin?' Saumya asked.

'Ashwin got married to that bloody backbencher, Rashmi. That son of a b***h was two-timing me!'

'And you got another dog and named it after him?' Saumya looked at Sweety, realizing she hadn't changed a bit in the last few weeks.

'Let's go,' Sweety said, changing the topic.

'Grow up, Sweety!' Saumya laughed.

7

'You understand, Mishraji. Why is Lallan so confused? It's not his fault,' said Subhash Jha, Lallan's father, clearing his throat.

'Meetu. You know her better, na? Topper, she is. I better find an engineer. I will give dowry up to twenty-five lakhs, but she is after me that she will only marry Lallan,' replied Meetu's father, B.K. Mishra.

The two friends were sitting across a vast table piled with *besan* laddus, *lavang latika*, *mattar* kachoris and *pyaaz* pakoras. Food is supposed to get two people close. But this massive spread did not bridge the gap in any way.

'I paid Lallan's dowry when he was ten. You know that.' Mishra was trying to score a point.

'I still feel obliged. He is alive because of that money. Otherwise I would be childless today,' Subhash Jha said soberly.

'When Kaali Pandey kidnapped Lallan, he was just ten. He could have done anything if I had not helped you to pay that ransom,' Mishra reminded him.

'Don't remind me again and again. I am obliged.' Jha had had his hands folded in obligation for the past ten years or so.

'So Kaali Pandey treats me like a servant on EMI and you want to treat me like a son-in-law on EMI?' questioned a young voice.

It was Lallan.

'Mishraji is not wrong, beta.' His father tried to negotiate peace.

'And yes, you didn't have forty lakhs to pay for my ransom; you just managed twenty, right? Mishra uncle gave the rest as pre-booking dowry!' Lallan was in no mood for peace.

'Have some respect at least,' Mishra spluttered. 'You have said *ulta-seedha* things to Meetu too. Her mother told me that she was crying all day long!'

'So tell me what I should do. I don't belong to myself. You own some stake because you paid 40 per cent of the ransom to free me. My father owns me as he paid another 40 per cent and Kaali owns me too as he gave a 20 per cent rebate!' Lallan sat on the punctured sofa with a helpless look on his face.

'Beta, we will find a way out.' The elder Jha patted his son on the back.

'No, there is no way out. I don't want to carry forward your bloody Jha Motor Driving School. I don't want to marry his unattractive, creepy, ever-clinging daughter. I don't want to be Kaali's remote-controlled toy!' Lallan began to cry.

Kids peeped over the boundary wall of his courtyard, listening to Lallan crying. Lallan felt like a butterfly caught in a fist. He picked up his Kotler book and rushed into his room.

He bolted the door and fell down on his bed with a thud. He wanted to fly. He wanted to fly very high, but could not. He wanted to break free of everyone's control, but could not. There was no way out. He had to change, eat and sleep.

By 4 a.m., he was back as a driving instructor. Sweety, whom he had known only as a silhouette, was now an unforgettable memory. He now knew her smell. He now knew her voice. He could not know only one thing. Why he couldn't hate her, as much as he hated her father? Why was it that her sandalwood smell didn't suffocate him? Why were her hands soft and not butcher-like like her father's? Why didn't he get affected by the company of his most hated enemy's daughter? The questions added to Lallan's circle of confusion.

8

4 a.m.

They saw each other again in the torchlight. He saw Sweety brighter and clearer than yesterday. They moved towards the red Maruti. Sweety was wearing a baby-pink tracksuit and a jacket. Lallan opened the door for her, got her seated in the driver's seat and locked the door. He then moved to the adjoining seat. It was a dark morning, a shade darker than the previous day.

'Seat belt,' Lallan reminded.

'Am I pretty?' she asked.

'Accelerator right side, break left,' Lallan changed the subject. 'Concentrate on the road and try to change the gear.' He was as stiff as possible.

'Topic diversion?' Sweety asked. She stopped the car and saw Ghonchu in the Jeep behind them. He was half asleep.

'Please start the car,' Lallan begged.

Sweety took the key out of the engine and started tossing it up and down in her hand.

'We are getting late,' said Lallan.

'Am I pretty?' Sweety asked again.

'I don't know,' Lallan muttered, glancing away.

'Get out of the car,' Sweety ordered.

'What do you want?' Lallan sounded defeated.

'Compliments!'

Lallan stared at her with a lot of curiosity. He noticed that her eyebrows met each other. He had rarely seen women with joined eyebrows.

'It's lucky!' she snapped.

'What?' Lallan tried to hide his embarrassment.

'My mom had the same eyebrows!' Sweety looked at herself in the dusty mirror.

Lallan didn't know what to say, what not to say, how to react and how not to react.

'Look at the way you maintain your car!' Sweety made a face, wiping off a little dust.

Lallan was amused. She was elemental in her mood swings. Lallan had never met someone like her. He had the daughter of the most hated man in his life sitting inches away and yet he did not hate her. This fact constantly alarmed him.

The horn blew like a trumpet from the Jeep following them. It was a lonely, quiet road outside the mansion premises. Some birds fluttered at the sound of the Jeep's horn.

'Please, I beg you, start the car.' Lallan looked back with an assurance that everything was all right.

'I haven't got my compliment yet!' Sweety reminded him.

'You are pretty,' Lallan said, discomfort clear on his face.

'Pretty like . . . ?' Sweety was playing around.

'Like . . . ?' Lallan stammered.

'I can't concentrate until I get my compliment.' Sweety started tapping the steering wheel.

'All right, you are pretty. Pretty like . . .' Lallan mumbled.

'Like? Come on. 1, 2, 3 . . .'

'Aishwarya Rai,' Lallan blurted out.

'Britney Spears,' Sweety corrected him.

She smiled and started the car.

They went around Kaali Pandey's mansion in the Maruti.

'It's going to be sunrise. We should end the class now,' Lallan insisted.

'This is just the beginning. I want to fly a helicopter one day!' Sweety declared dreamily.

'You know you are punishing me for your dream,' Lallan said bleakly.

'You hate waking up early?' asked Sweety.

'I have my exams. I will fail.'

'What are you studying?'

'MBA.'

'Hmm.' Sweety felt bad.

'I want to become a big businessman!' Lallan had the same dreamy look.

'I thought you worked on and off for Papa,' Sweety said.

'It's a long story, one which has cut my dreams short,' said Lallan.

The fraction of a second they looked into each other's eyes was truly magical. It was like a shooting star had just crossed their eyes. Ghonchu was already there to open the door. Neither Lallan nor Sweety said goodbye.

9

Britney Spears, he Googled, as she tried to peep into his HCL notebook. This was the cheapest gadget Meetu had gifted him on his birthday.

Meetu had made a love proposal on a PPT and surprised him. That was one of the stupidest moments for Lallan's diary.

'Britney Spears?' teased Meetu.

'Don't try to peep in. It's private,' warned Lallan.

Lallan was lying on a cot in the courtyard with his laptop like a tray on his lap.

'Private, haan?' Meetu knew no boundaries when it came to teasing him.

'What happened? Why are you here?' asked Lallan in a curt voice.

'Hello . . . Papa is retiring . . . I have come to invite you all. There is a small function at his office.' Meetu pretended to be businesslike. She extended the white postcard–sized invitation. Meetu was there to invite the whole family for 'Vidai Samaroh' of her father.

'Give it to Papa. What will I do?' Lallan pointed towards the drawing room where his father was busy reading a newspaper.

'Why are you looking for Britney Spears, by the way?' Meetu teased him again.

Lallan didn't want to answer and tried to ignore her.

'You like modern dresses, don't you?' she enquired.

'I have to leave.' Lallan got up. He was in no mood to get into an unnecessarily steamy conversation with Meetu. She could steam up like an espresso machine whenever and wherever. Lallan wanted to avoid that. Meetu held his hand tightly.

'I can wear a swimsuit for you! Just say yes!' Her gaze drilled deep into his eyes.

'Are there no other guys in Patna? Spare me please,' Lallan whispered as he pulled his wrist out of her grip.

'You know how much I love you. Let's get married. Stop insulting me now and then. I give you so much bhaav; no one would ever do so.'

'I will find a better guy for you. I am jobless, eating out of my father's business. Kaali Pandey uses me like his doormat all the time. Why do you want to marry a guy like me?' Lallan's frustration came forth.

'We will go to Mumbai . . . Delhi . . . anywhere, after our shaadi.' Meetu behaved as if she wasn't listening.

'Kaali will have to set me free for that. He had let me go on a discounted ransom when I was ten, only on the condition that I will serve him until I turn forty.' Lallan could not control his angst.

Meetu tried to take out the knots from his stiff shoulder. 'Tiger balm . . . Should I apply some?' she asked the fiery Lallan. He tried to brush her hands off.

Lallan's mother was there with a plate of baingan and aloo and a sharp knife. Meetu handed her the invite.

'Baingan aloo. I am making it with the *vadi* we had made together,' Lallan's mother said, looking at Meetu with a warm smile to compensate for his misbehaviour. Meetu and his mother stood together, appreciating the freshness of the baingan.

Lallan moved away with his notebook. He always wanted to move away from this world.

'This notebook has become old. Shall I get you an iPad on your birthday? Do you like the mini one?' asked Meetu, seeing her Superman storming off. She got no acknowledgement, as always.

10

Sweety and Saumya were cheering themselves up and bringing on the late night with hot chocolate.

'I researched about him . . . Bechara.' Sweety looked very sad.

'Uncle? Who knows him better than you?' Saumya tried explaining stuff to Sweety.

'I hate Papa. He can be so rude, so selfish. I am ashamed that he is my father!'

Saumya held Sweety's hands to comfort her. 'At times, I feel that it would have been better if I had been left in some garbage bin. At least I would have been on my own.'

'Fate, destiny—you believe in it, don't you?' Saumya caressed her fingers.

'I have seen this guy. Not properly though.' Sweety went back to talking about Lallan.

'Lallan, the driver?' Saumya asked.

'He is not a driver, yaar. He is doing his MBA in Uncle's institute. Bechara, he is like me. He too can't move out of Patna. Papa has claimed his services till he turns forty.'

'So Ghonchu told you his story?' asked Saumya.

'No. The new servant. The thin one,' said Sweety. She had so much to say. 'Papa had kidnapped him when he was barely ten years old. His family could not give the full ransom. Papa generously gave some rebate but claimed him till he turns forty for his illegal jobs. He uses him for his illegal small-time smuggling, etc. What's his fault?' Sweety felt sorry for him. 'Can you believe that because of my driving lessons he cannot study and might fail? I am feeling miserable, yaar.'

'You can help him out. Don't go for driving classes till his exams are over!' Saumya advised.

'I should get his number.'

'Aren't you getting too concerned about him?' asked Saumya.

'He is not a bad guy.'

'It's a mess. I am warning you. Stay away from him. I think you have developed some liking for him.' Saumya tried to find out the truth.

'I just know that I am waiting for my next driving lesson,' said Sweety, guzzling down the hot chocolate. She loosened her ponytail to let her hair breathe. She rested her head on the fluffy, lavender pillow. Saumya got up to wear her jacket.

'Hope you have closed your old chapter?' asked Saumya.

'Long back.' Sweety was quick.

'I know you never close your chapters so easily, Sweety. Just advising you to stay away from everything,' Saumya warned.

'I have nothing left, baba. Papa didn't let me go out of Patna to study. On top of it, he has threatened me. He has caged me here. I don't know how long this imprisonment will last.' Sweety looked at the ceiling, at the whirling fan.

Saumya bent down and pulled Sweety's cheeks.

'I have to leave . . . have a flight tomorrow'.

Sweety sulked. Saumya kissed her on her forehead.

'And, yes, delete all old numbers from your mobile.' Saumya walked towards the door. She always had a bucketful of advice.

'You enjoy your life in Delhi. Party, fun, *aish*! I will be here with my dogs and Hitler.' Sweety bid a cranky farewell to Saumya. Saumya smiled her angelic smile and left quickly.

Pillows become your best friends—you hug them, kiss them, wet them with your tears, mumble your deepest feelings and bury your tantrums in them. Sweety's pillow was her secret best friend, after Saumya.

11

Lallan smiled, looking at the little signage at a counter in the bank: 'May I help you?'

'Business loan. What is the procedure?' asked Lallan, with diffidence.

'What's your business proposal, sir?' the bank executive asked in return.

'Insurance,' Lallan replied.

'Okay. Do you have a detailed business proposal?' The woman flash-scanned him. The thing with these bank executives is that they are trained to scan you without you realizing it. They assess you even before they check your status or account. Lallan handed over a file.

'It's a unique business idea. No one has ever done it before. It will change the market dynamics. Nothing like this has happened before,' Lallan said loudly.

Some people have derived a unique mode of conversation. They never believe in talking softly or gently. They think that their speech volume is directly proportional to convincing power. The higher you go, the greater the probability of a hit!

The executive was wearing a red-orange sari and had put on her bright, charged-up face with the armour of fresh morning make-up. She looked like a Bharatanatyam dancer. As she went through the file, her mouth fell open. Then she looked at Lallan in utter disbelief. Her colleague, who was sitting next to her, understood that here was something interesting! He took the file from her and flipped through it. From the corner of his eyes, he looked at Mr Lallan Jha, the applicant with this interesting proposal. Lallan's discomfort was evident.

'The nearest mental hospital is in an area called Kanke, which is in Ranchi. Ranchi is the capital city of Jharkhand. It's about nine hundred and fifty kilometres away. And if you think you are not comfortable in a hospital nearby then you will have to go a bit further. I think Agra would be the best place in your case.' He slammed the business proposal file in front of Lallan.

'I can explain. Believe me. It will work wonders!' Lallan tried to convince the man.

'And our bank will certainly sponsor your mad dream. Oh, yes!' the executive said sarcastically.

'This is a perfect insurance model for the kind of mishaps taking place on a day-to-day basis in our state. A perfect model for Bihar. I have my research in place too. When it can be done in many countries, why can't we introduce and implement this here?' Lallan argued.

By now, all the employees had gathered around him. The guards were also prepared to throw him away.

'Brazil, Mexico, Nigeria—when they can do it, why can't we?' Lallan had done his research.

'Kidnapping insurance!' the executive shouted.

'Yes, kidnapping insurance!' Lallan asserted.

Lallan was eventually thrown out. The employees looked at each other.

'Google!' the male executive told the lady.

Lallan was not wrong. A page on kidnapping insurance opened. The employees looked at each other in surprise. Kidnapping insurance was Lallan's dream.

12

'Ow . . . Don't pull off my skin,' screamed Sweety. Her beautician had come home. She was getting a chocolate arm wax. The beautician rubbed an ice cube on her skin. 'Listen . . . Do something with my hair,' insisted Sweety.

'Streaks?' asked the beautician.

'No! Something drastic!' Sweety had a spark in her eyes. She got up and got her iPad and searched for the crazy-coloured styles of Britney Spears, Lady Gaga, Madonna, etc. 'You know, something like this!' She pointed at a picture of Britney Spears in purple hair with a puppy cut on her forehead.

'This is Patna, Sweety didi. People will laugh at you and your style. This is not Hollywood,' the beautician tried to explain to Sweety.

'As if I give a damn.' Sweety looked at her with raised eyebrows.

'Whatever you say. I was just giving some advice,' the beautician toned down to show her indifference.

'Get going then!' Sweety always flagged off things. Ordering people around was in her genes.

'Are you sure?' the beautician reconfirmed.

'Sweety decides only once!'

So, on Sweety's insistence, her experiment began! She got a fringe; got the chemicals fizzing in her hair; and the hair turned purple in no time. She knew that her father would boil when he saw this new look. Deep inside she wanted to hurt her father in as many juvenile ways as possible.

Sweety was never afraid to look new and weird. She faced the mirror with a smile. 'What if Patna doesn't like it!' Then she tipped the beautician a five hundred–rupee note. The beautician dutifully kept it in her blouse and started packing the chaos which was spread all over in the name of beauty.

Sweety was soaking in self-love. She picked up the remote of her sound system and played Britney Spears number, 'I wanna go', loud. She didn't even acknowledge the beautician leaving.

When she finally looked in the mirror, the self-obsessed Sweety saw her giant father standing tall behind her. She turned around. Kaali Pandey slapped her. Sweety smiled.

'Who will marry you?' shouted Kaali.

'I will choose my guy; the guy will not choose me!' Sweety retorted.

'Have you gone mad?' Kaali was trying to control his spiralling anger.

'Anybody would go mad. No one can be sane in this caged life,' Sweety shouted back.

'So, this entire rebellion is happening because you want me to allow you to go out of Patna?'

'What do you care?' Sweety shrugged.

This annoyed Kaali Pandey. He held her by her shoulder and shook her. 'I care . . . That's why I have kept you in protection. The elections are going to start soon. You know I have got threats. You are my most precious possession. I can't let your life be in danger!' Kaali Pandey spoke rapidly.

'I took part in the Pop Queen Hunt audition. I was the only contestant to be finalized from Patna. But you didn't let me go to Mumbai. You killed my dreams!' Sweety said angrily.

'You lied to me. I never even knew that you had gone for an audition. I have given you a free hand; that's my fault,' Kaali said remorsefully.

'Lies and lies! That's the way to deal with a father like you,' Sweety gave it back to him.

'Sweety, I am your father. I have raised you since childhood, after your ma . . .' he stuttered.

'Ma?' questioned Sweety looking directly into his eyes, killing him with a hateful look.

'We will talk tomorrow.' Kaali turned to leave.

Sweety blocked him. 'Ma . . . what . . . ?'

Kaali was silent.

'Ma committed suicide. She didn't die. You killed her. Your terror compelled her to kill herself!'

Kaali was still silent.

'You haven't shed a tear yet. You are the dreaded don! Now a reputed politician. Outlaw-turned-lawmaker. You are an expert in legitimizing all your illegal jobs now. You think no one can touch you ever!' Sweety mocked. Kaali stood, without any reaction, against his daughter's tirade. 'You took away her life and now you will take mine!'

Kaali held her tightly against his chest. Sweety continued to weep like a child.

In her purple hair and puppy-cut fringes, she looked like a rebel doll lost in her wonderland.

Sweety's eyes were swollen and red. Her cheeks had turned pink. She wanted to hug her pillow, her best friend, and bury all her pain inside it. She didn't want to break down in front of Kaali Pandey. She always reacted and gave him back, but today the tears had to flow. A long and deep storage of memories, grief, pain and complains. Sweety was, in fact, a lonely, motherless child.

Her mother had committed suicide when she was just four years old. Her mother dealt a lot with her moral turmoil of being married to a man who was heading a ruthless kidnapping mafia. She knew that nothing would set things right. She'd seen the inside of a criminal life. She tolerated things till she could. When she could not bear it any more, she left the little girl and a one-line suicide note, which read, 'Take care of my daughter, if you ever loved me.'

Sweety's mother's younger brother had been kidnapped and killed by a rival kidnapping gang. This kidnapping ring was headed by Radhey Shyam Yadav. He was from a village called Badka Gaon in Motihari District of Bihar. In the initial days of their career in the kidnapping industry, Kaali Pandey and Radhey Shyam Yadav used to be partners in crime. Their business flourished to a great level until, one day, a misunderstanding tore their relationship apart. The gap between them had only widened with the passage of time. When Kaali Pandey's brother-in-law was kidnapped and killed, and his wife had committed suicide, it was a moment of realization for him. He had then decided to take a plunge into a crime-free life. Kaali had begun with small crimes and then graduated to bigger ones. Now his next step was to work in the area of legitimizing all his illegal work, and that would not be possible without actually becoming a part of the lawmaking bodies. He decided to join politics. He won the next local elections and has been winning all assembly polls since. He was a minister now.

But the stain and the scars remained and often came back to haunt him.

13

It was 4 a.m. again. Lallan was at the doorstep. He had his Philip Kotler in his hand. He had to rush for his exams after the driving class. Ghonchu was sitting half asleep on a cane chair. There was no trace of Sweety.

'Must be getting ready,' Ghonchu told Lallan.

Lallan walked across the veranda. It was misty and cold.

'How is Sweety learning?' Ghonchu asked Lallan.

'Ya . . . Good . . . fine,' Lallan praised in his own unsure way as always.

Lallan waited. Ten minutes. Twenty minutes. Thirty minutes.

He waited for the torchlight to blind him. That's the way Sweety said hello to him.

'Can you check?' Lallan asked Ghonchu.

The mouse-looking servant came out just then with a little chit in Sweety's legible writing.

```
Sorry. I don't want to bother you. I
don't want to learn to drive. I don't
want to trouble you, waking you up
at 4 a.m. Best of luck for your paper,
dear businessman!
```

Ghonchu tried to read by jumping in to see the letter.

'It's in English,' said Lallan.

Ghonchu ordered with authority, 'Translate in Hindi.'

'Sorry. Mujhe driving nahi seekhni hai,' read Lallan.

'That's it? It was a very long sentence in English.' Ghonchu had his own conclusions.

Lallan should have felt relieved and better. But, no, that was not the case. He felt the exact opposite. He felt that something was amiss here. He felt a little heavy. Lallan took a pen out from his pocket. He searched for a paper and, in a hurry, took his Philip Kotler and tore a corner from the last page. He scribbled something and gave it to the servant.

'What are you writing?' Ghonchu enquired seriously.

Lallan said politely, 'Nothing. Just saying thanks.'

Ghonchu said, 'Okay,' in his squeaky uncultured voice.

Lallan scribbled something.

'It's taking so much time to write a "thank you"?' Ghonchu got curious again. He was behaving like an ISI agent.

'Long thank you,' said Lallan smilingly and wrapped the chit and handed it over to the servant before Ghonchu could intervene any further. The servant took the chit and went inside.

Sweety was in her room, on the bed, quietly fiddling with her alarm clock like a toy.

'Sweety didi . . . chit . . . Lallan,' muttered the servant.

Sweety took the chit.

```
Hi, thanks. By the way, I lied to you.
Sorry about that. My Aishwarya Rai
compliment was wrong! You don't look
that plastic. Your smile is real. Real
and very special!—Lallan.
```

Nobody had ever flirted so honestly with Sweety Pandey in her entire life. Sweety's face bloomed like a lily. She ran to the French window with the lavender drapes. She picked up her torch and flashed it right across the lane, where the red Maruti was still standing there. Lallan was getting in to go back. She adjusted the spotlight like a professional camerawoman and it fell on Lallan's round face. Lallan's forehead shone. He blinked.

There was an interesting difference between the two girls, Sweety and Meetu, in their choice of men. Meetu, like many other girls in the Hindi heartland, would fall in line with the feudal value system where the man would be the master of the house. He would be dominating. Masculinity would be reaffirmed and reinsured. The concept of a metrosexual man was unheard in that category of girls. If they saw a guy inside the periphery of his home for a long period of time, he would be termed a *mauga*. The term mauga is used as a negative version of the sociological term metrosexual, to describe guys with an interest in the domestic chores, transcending the conservative norms of the society.

But for the likes of Sweety, the woman being on the top had nothing to do with these modern and postmodern sociological terms. It simply questioned why the man should always take the lead. Sweety never wished for a Superman.

Unlike Meetu, Sweety preferred a helpless man to a Superman.

Lallan couldn't see the source of the light. Everything was pitch-dark. He wanted to figure out, but he was hesitant and conscious at the same time. Sweety could sense uneasiness on his face. She turned the torch to her face, making it shine brighter and more beautiful like a full moon. She smiled. He was ecstatic. His superfast heartbeats reminded him of the Patna Rajdhani.

It was a moment of light and love for Sweety and Lallan who were some distance apart. The distance was simply geographical.

A hide-and-seek game of love had just begun.

14

It was his toughest examination till date. Lallan was writing research and marketing exam. He was sitting in the right corner of the exam hall, next to the window. The light coming from the sun reminded him of the torchlight that had swept his face, every day at four in the morning.

Lallan was trying to concentrate, but Sweety's torch-lit smile was dancing in front of his eyes, on loop.

'One more bell to go!' announced one of the invigilators.

At BBGIM, staff members were generally the bored wives of bureaucrats. The invigilator was Ms Alka Shrivastava in a baby-pink silk sari and was decked in diamond jewellery.

The baby-pink colour of her sari reminded him of the baby-pink tracksuit and jacket Sweety had worn for her second driving lesson. Her sandalwood smell was such a charm. It filled up the little car and, to an extent, his heart and memories, beating even Philip Kotler!

It was a profound thought indeed that just as the lotus blooms in the dirt, the dirt and muck that was Kaali Pandey had borne a beautiful pink lotus.

Sweety studied in the best convent school of Patna, spoke fluent English, rolled her tongue like soft pizza dough when needed. She was beautiful; her temper and mood swings added to her charm. She was spontaneous and vibrant. Unlike Kaali, she was not ruthless. The note she had sent to Lallan reflected that she had a heart. She did care for the people around her. She was loving by nature.

Lallan was affected. In fact, infected.

'Only ten minutes,' the invigilator reminded the students.

Lallan was racing against time. He tried to write faster. It felt like he was swimming against the tide. Images of Sweety were floating around him; he was trying to hold on to his sanity.

The final bell rang. The invigilator appeared the way Anil Kapoor does after switching off his gadget in Shekhar Kapoor's *Mr India*, to take away the paper. Lallan did not want to deposit his answer paper as yet. He instantly felt a strong sense of possessiveness for his answer paper. He wanted to write more. He was holding on to it, close to his chest. The invigilator tried to snatch the paper. Lallan was not ready to give in and started a tug of war that resulted in tearing of Lallan's answer sheet.

The whole class went into a coma. Even the invigilator was in a state of deep guilt. He instructed the peon to get some cellophane tape and a pair of scissors from the office and then, with his help, tried to reattach all the pages of the answer book. Lallan was in tears and the invigilator was also troubled. There was pin-drop silence in the whole class.

'I am extremely sorry. You could not complete all your answers in time,' said the invigilator.

'Don't worry, sir. There is no end to the stories wrought out on paper. If not today, someday else,' replied Lallan.

The invigilator was shocked at Lallan's response. If he was not writing serious answers, why was he refusing to part with his answer sheet even after the time was over, he wondered.

Lallan Jha's style of taking this sort of non-seriousness so seriously was beyond the comprehension of all his teachers in the business school. Lallan looked disappointed. Meetu was sitting five seats behind him. Picking up his bag, he walked out, when Meetu approached him. Road-blocking was her favourite game.

'Pass?' she asked Lallan.

'You?' asked Lallan.

'With distinction,' Meetu replied.

Lallan kept on walking. Meetu rallied.

'You know, Lallan, it's written on your face that you hate me, but I still want to tell you one thing. Dreams are dreams. You always dream beyond your shoe size. To become a business tycoon, to marry Aishwarya Rai . . .'

'I don't like Aishwarya Rai.'

'Oh, until three days ago, you were watching her films back to back—*Hum Dil De Chuke Sanam, Guzarish, Josh, Devdas* . . .' Meetu teased.

'Tastes change.' Lallan smiled.

'Did you just smile?' Meetu was in front of him, scrutinizing his face.

'What?' Lallan pretended not to understand.

'You smiled! It has been ages since I saw you smile!' Meetu looked at him in surprise.

'You want to eat chhola bhatura?' asked Lallan, trying to change the topic.

'I must be dreaming,' said Meetu.

'Come to the canteen.' Lallan walked ahead.

Meetu was confused to see Lallan become so friendly suddenly. She walked behind him in quick steps till the canteen. They ate the chhola bhatura with relish.

'You know, I don't feel good about myself when I look into the mirror. There is nothing special about me. What do you like in me?' Lallan asked her. He wanted to know more about himself. He wanted to cross-examine his own worth. Lallan always enjoyed dissecting his own personality. He was somewhere between being a self-indulgent guy and a megalomaniac, though he would never express any of this explicitly.

'You are clean at heart,' said Meetu, licking the aloo in the chholey. A piece of aloo in the chholey is as precious as a diamond in your jewellery box.

'Heart? Who knows what is there in someone's heart? It's all bullshit!' Lallan had a slightly shrewd smile on his face.

'It's not bullshit. I know what you are and how you are. It's not easy to get a guy like you. You underestimate yourself,' said Meetu.

Lallan looked at Meetu for a second. Meetu's heart skipped a beat. Not one but many!

'Really?' smiled Lallan.

Lallan was in love. Absolute love! His heart was hanging from the barbed, jagged wire of hatred. He was in love with the daughter of a man he loathed.

'I have been meeting everyone for my business to be funded. No one cares. They laugh at me!' Lallan dropped his smile.

'You can do something else. Maybe join a bank. There are so many private banks. You will get a good salary, AC office—' Meetu tried negotiating his dream plan.

'No. I am born to be an entrepreneur. I don't want to do *chindi naukri* all my life—work twelve hours a day. I want to rise, expand, shine and make a mark!' Lallan had so much to say about his dream.

'But kidnapping insurance? Don't you have a better business idea than this?' Meetu asked him point blank.

'You know what, will you mind if I tell you a story to explain my mind better?' asked Lallan.

'Why would I? In fact, I would love to know you more, inside out.' Meetu was excited.

'There was a very famous shoe-manufacturing company. The company was very successful in selling its products wherever it used to sell. Like every other successful company this one also wanted to expand its market to new regions. The company spotted two of its best marketing professionals and assigned them something very interesting as well as challenging. The company sent both of them to some remote place in Africa which was never in any news or tourism map. The company wanted them to do first-hand research about a possible shoe market in those areas in Africa . . .' Lallan started narrating a story.

Meetu rarely got time and attention from him. She indulged.

'The company management receives a telegram from the first marketing professional just in two days: *I'm coming back shortly as I've come to a place where no one wears footwear and there is no culture to cover your feet while stepping out of your house. There is no scope to sell shoes over here. This whole exercise was a complete waste of time.*

Meetu was engrossed in Lallan's narration.

'The company management was curious to get a feedback from the second marketing guy who had gone incommunicado.

There was no news from him for a month or so. The shoe manufacturers received a telegram from him five weeks after he had gone for his research. He had written: *Sending you an order for ten lakh pairs of shoes. I have come to a place where no one uses footwear and there is no culture and practice to cover your feet while stepping out of your house. So I envision an immense possibility for sales of our product by developing a culture of covering everyone's feet while they walk out of their home. It's a wonderful market with a lot of potential and we can get the first mover advantage for our product.*

Meetu listened to Lallan, understanding the point he was trying to make.

'Both the guys had gone to the same place, but the way they looked at things changed the way things turned out to be,' said Lallan.

'So, you want to be the second man.' Meetu wanted to prove her intelligence. These chances were few and far between.

'Yes. I don't want a mediocre life. I want to be one amongst the Tatas, Birlas, Ambanis . . .' Lallan's chest expanded with pride.

His phone rang. It was Ghonchu.

'Saheb asked you to go to Kala Qila and get five lakhs from Naathu Singh,' ordered Ghonchu like a commando. Kala Qila, unlike Lal Qila, was a den in the empire of Kaali Pandey where all his payments from the illegal selling of arms and ammunitions would get collected from his munshi Naathu Singh.

'By evening,' said Lallan.

'In ten minutes,' challenged Ghonchu.

'Okay,' Lallan grumbled.

Lallan got up. He was not the same man. He did not look distressed. He looked all geared up for it.

'What happened?' Meetu already knew what it is.

'See! I am living life like a soldier and not serving the country—serving Kaali Pandey.' He tried to be gallant in front of Meetu.

Lallan picked up his bag, drank a bottle of water and wiped his oily hands with a tissue.

'We have to talk more. A glass of lassi is due,' said Meetu, who was pretty unhappy with the half conversation.

The canteen waiter was there with the bill. Lallan handed over a hundred-rupee note and left. Meetu sat by looking at the leftovers on her plate. A long, slit green chilli stared back at her. Lallan was an unsolved puzzle for her. He was like a tough round of Sudoku. The more she wanted to attempt solving it, the more she got confused. And now she saw her puzzle walking away, unsolved. Yet again!

15

'This election, we have to again come to power,' Kaali Pandey told his gathered allies.

'Radhey Shyam Yadav has got his wife nominated to contest against you,' said one of the party members.

'Making gol rotis and policy are two completely different things,' Kaali mocked.

'They have minority vote bank!' told another party member.

'We will buy votes. We will bribe them to vote. We just need money,' Kaali ordered.

'There is strict surveillance this time . . . we must be very careful,' the first member warned Kaali again.

'Everything is fair in love, war and elections!' declared Kaali.

He got up to leave. Ghonchu stood at his side like an alert dog.

'Radhey Shyam will be nothing in front of me.' Kaali Pandey looked confident.

'We are getting funding from a lot of businessmen. It does not look to be enough though,' stated another party member.

'Put Lallan on a collection spree. Send him the list quickly.' Kaali turned towards Ghonchu. 'Did you ask him to get the *peti* from Kala Qila?'

Ghonchu nodded.

'Good! His image is clean. He is not a *gunda mawali*. He doesn't create scenes. We need to have youth like him to get our work done in a sober way,' Kaali explained.

Kaali shuffled out of the room. His darbar was adjourned and everyone dismissed. Kaali's cavalcade had just left. The mansion was lonely for some seconds. A bike stopped. It was Lallan with a plastic bag, *Jalaan Sattu evam Besan* imprinted on it. He had gotten the petis he was supposed to get from the munshi. The bag was not that heavy. Five petis is humbly equal to the weight of five kilos of mutton.

He stepped inside the mansion. There was nobody, for a change. The meek servant came to attend to Lallan.

'Ghonchu?' asked Lallan.

'Urgent work. He has gone with Saheb.'

Lallan was a little unsure.

'Anyone else?'

'Only Sweety didi,' said the servant.

'Can you call her?' asked Lallan.

'No. You can give it to me. Saheb has given me permission to collect,' said the servant.

Lallan was still pretty unsure. He was still contemplating when Sweety came down the stairs.

'Give it to him; he will keep it safely in my room. Don't worry,' Sweety assured.

Lallan's hand was shaking, as Sweety came closer to him. He handed the bag to the servant.

'You know where to keep it?' Sweety asked the servant. He took the hint and went upstairs.

Sweety and Lallan were alone for the first time. Lallan's heart beat fast. He felt like a culprit to have thought of Sweety every passing second, pushing Philip Kotler to a distant second in his arrangement of thoughts.

'Rooh Afza?' asked Sweety.

Lallan didn't move. She went to the dining room and, from a small fridge kept in the corner, pulled out two bottles. One was Rooh Afza and the other was water. She stirred in some red sherbet and gave it to Lallan. Lallan was still all ice and cold sweat after such a close encounter.

'You don't need ice, I guess; you look frozen.' Sweety smiled at him.

'No, I am okay . . . perfectly okay.' Lallan tried to maintain his composure.

'Sit.' Sweety's requests and orders were slightly confusing for others.

'Drink; it's really nice,' she said.

Lallan gulped down a huge mouthful.

'How was your exam?' asked Sweety.

'I think I should pass.'

'You listen to music?'

'Yes . . . Haan,' said Lallan, still sweating in uneasiness. He was sitting on the sofa he had never dared to sit on before.

Sweety picked up a guitar kept beside the sofa and sat across him.

'English medium or Hindi medium?' asked Sweety.

'Hindi.'

Sweety smiled and started strumming the guitar. She looked like Parveen Babi with the guitar and a maxi dress. Yes she was playing the notes of 'Churaliya hai tumne jo dil ko, Nazar nahi churana sanam.' Sweety started humming. She did not sing with the lyrics. Instead she jammed with a hum, while strumming on her guitar.

Lallan was in awe. He had never seen a sight as mesmerizing as this. A stunningly beautiful girl, the only daughter of the deadliest mafia kingpin of his time, was smoothly playing a guitar in a graveyard of a mansion. How could she be so attractive, so cute, so beautiful, so diva-like? It was mind-blowing. Lallan was lost. He was forgetting his discomfort.

Sweety finished on a high note, staring deep into Lallan's eyes.

'You are wow!' said Lallan.

'I sing English better,' Sweety patted herself.

'I must go.' Lallan got up in a hurry. He knew that whatever happiness he was experiencing would be a disaster if somebody got wind of it.

'Let's become friends, Lallan Jha,' Sweety invited him in her husky voice.

'My exams get over this week. Let's restart the driving classes,' said Lallan, sounding confident for the first time, even if it was all pretention.

'I don't want to use you like a toy the way my father does.' Sweety looked at him intensely.

'Your driver will see you sharp at 4 a.m. . . . . from Monday,' Lallan announced.

His Rooh Afza glass was empty by now.

'Tell me more about your business plan, the next time we meet,' Sweety said as Lallan prepared to leave.

'You sing the English one, next time we meet.' Lallan's face reddened.

'You know our friendship can be dangerous,' Sweety warned him with a smile.

'Your father has trained me to play with danger.' Lallan had a counter-smile on his face.

Seeing a brave Lallan was a sight in itself. They looked at each other for a few seconds longer. Lallan walked towards the door. Sweety sat still with her guitar. They said no byes, but their eyes met each other and spoke volumes!

Lallan had gone. Sweety stood there with her guitar and the empty glass of the love drink—Rooh Afza!

16

That night was a terrible, irresistible night. Sweety was awake. It was past midnight. She had a bowl of Maggi in front of her. She was eating less, playing more.

Sweety loved midnight munchies. It was a bowl of Maggi mostly. That was the only thing she knew how to cook. She added a dollop of butter when she wanted to treat herself. The next morning used to be a regretful one. Sweety wanted to be in shape, her dream shape, Britney Spears shape!

A girl who is up past midnight with a bowl of Maggi needs a companion to share things with. She was feeling lonely. She was in a dilemma whether to call Saumya or not. She thought for few seconds and then called her up.

A long ring. A long caller tune at the other side. 'Hmmm,' said Saumya, picking up the call.

'You miss me?' Sweety asked her.

'No, no, no, baba. I have made many friends here. I am partying . . . in a disco,' Saumya tried to tease her in her lazy, sleepy voice.

'Listen. Ask your papa for a favour,' said Sweety.

'What?' asked Saumya.

'That guy, Lallan . . . he should not fail. Ask Gupta uncle to do something, na,' Sweety pleaded.

'I can predict the future,' said Saumya.

'What?' asked Sweety innocently..

'Very soon, you will have a new dog named Lallan,' teased Saumya.

'You are taking my case, na?' Sweety pretended to be angry.

'No, baba, I am just warning you to not kid around any more. Uncle is in another frame of mind. His elections are approaching,' Saumya tried to drill some sense into her bestie.

'So?' Sweety wanted to hear more of the consequences from her friend's mouth.

'So? You are asking me, so?'

Sweety was silent.

'You know he will get you married to any Tom, Dick or Harry if he gets to know that you are in love with his slave,' Saumya told her clearly.

'He isn't his slave,' Sweety corrected her.

'Oh, stop kidding. You know your father better than that!' Saumya explained again.

Saumya's patience fluctuated but she could never be angry with Sweety. One moment she might be instructive with her but the other moment she would balance it with her angelic smile.

'I got it. And I think you are over-reading. I am not in love with this guy. I was actually a bit concerned. He looks so bechara to me.' Sweety cleared her court.

'Sweety, Sweety Pandey, getting sensitive towards a guy! That's quite a story!' Saumya laughed.

'I also have a large heart,' Sweety stated with pride.

'Good night. Sleep tight now.' Saumya bid a farewell to Sweety with a long-distance kiss.

Sweety held her inanimate best friend, her pillow tightly. She brushed her face against it. She opened her tightly held hair in a ponytail. Her hair fell all over her face, framing it beautifully.

*

It was a roller-coaster night for Lallan too. He did not eat his dinner. Lallan had this habit of losing his appetite when he was in his dreamy stage. The image of Sweety with a guitar in her arms, humming 'churaliya hai tumne' was coming back to haunt him again and again.

His heart had only had space for his dreams of becoming an entrepreneur. He could feel Sweety slowly creeping into his dream space. It was truly like a dream sequence for him. His Philip Kotler book lay in a corner of his bed. Lallan didn't feel like touching it today.

He was still swimming in the Rooh Afza which Sweety served him with love. The nude bulb hanging loosely on the wall stared at Lallan. Lallan stared back at the lamp. Sandalwood aroma filled his nostrils again. The nude lamp was like the sun their love story had never seen. They always met in darkness and the light of love seemed to be far away.

Thoughts of Sweety's joint eyebrows, the cleft on her chin and her black eyes kept him awake. Lallan was busy biting his nails. He was completely baffled. He took out the day's newspaper and started solving the Sudoku puzzle. This was the era of phones, WhatsApp and Facebook, but Lallan didn't have any connect with Sweety. He should have got her number at least. He should have given his number at least. How could he wait for Monday?

He had hated it when he had gotten a call from Ghonchu to come and teach Sweety driving. He had felt like a slave but he had not imagined things would take a turn like this. Now, he felt free for the first time. Sweety's free soul had bestowed him with a dangerous, almost suicidal, sense of freedom. He wondered how she was such a free and lively soul living in an imposing mansion like that.

Both Lallan and Sweety tossed and turned on their beds all night. Symptoms of love were evident! The sun rose like a poached egg in a pan. It looked beautiful. It looked like a little roundel of love.

17

The much anticipated Monday finally arrived.

At 4 a.m., Kaali Pandey's mansion flickered in the small night lamp on the main gate. Sweety came out holding a torch. She looked much brighter today. She was in a grey tracksuit but still looked brighter than she had looked in pink. Love does that to you. Lallan was inside the car. He got down and opened the door for her.

The ever-yawning Ghonchu walked to the Jeep in a half-asleep state. With all the chivalry, Lallan shut the door after Sweety got into the car. Sweety sat and, without insistence, put on the seat belt. Lallan sat beside her and adjusted his seat, so that he was shoulder to shoulder with Sweety.

'Good girl, na?' she said gesturing towards the seat belt. Lallan smiled. Sweety was in a very accommodative mood today. She played these little tantrum games. No one could figure out her mood at any point of time.

'Should I tell you about the gears once again?' Lallan asked her.

'Sweety is not that dumb. I remember very well.' Sweety started the car and shifted to the first gear.

The Jeep refused to start due to some congestion issue, despite Ghonchu's repeated attempts. He repeatedly failed to ignite the engine. Sweety could see all this in the rear-view mirror. Ghonchu tried to wave a hand to stop. Instead of halting, she shifted to the second gear. Ghonchu quickly opened the bonnet of his Jeep for a quick inspection. He looked clueless.

'I think we should stop.' Lallan could sense the situation. He realized that they were moving ahead, unguarded, and that was threatening.

'Once Sweety starts, she doesn't stop.' Sweety shifted into third gear and her car sped with a vroom. This was the first time she was driving so fast.

'Control . . . easy.' Lallan tried to calm her down.

Sweety braked at the dead end of the road. It was quite a distance from Kaali Pandey's mansion and deadly surveillance. In her rear-view mirror, she could see a man panting and running in the distance. It was Ghonchu and he was far, far off. He was anyhow dragging himself to run behind the car.

It was still dark. Nothing was visible. Sweety and Lallan were alone inside the tiny, hundred-square-foot shell of the red Maruti. The headlights blinked. They looked at each other. Mist blanketed the rolled-up windows of the car. The streetlights were in a haze. Low voltage kept them in a sleepy mode. These streetlights were no brighter than lanterns.

'I am scared,' said Lallan.

He tried looking here and there, trying to make sense of the situation. He was in the radar of the mighty man whose threat grew as he grew older. And he was with his young, beautiful and crazy daughter.

'A Leo . . . and scared?' asked Sweety.

'How do you know that I am a Leo?' Lallan was inquisitive.

'Sweety can never like a Ram . . . You have to be a Leo,' she smiled.

Lallan was sweating, his forehead all dewed. The tender leaves outside, in the summery morning, were dancing over with dew drops. Nature was conspiring to create the perfect moment. Lallan tried to be firm but his hands trembled.

'Are you a Ram?' she challenged Lallan.

'No,' he said.

'Then grab your tigress.'

Transfixed, Lallan could not move even an inch. Sweety came closer to him and held him by his collar.

'Ghonchu—' muttered Lallan.

'Is far away . . . very far,' encouraged Sweety.

Lallan's trembling hands held her by the nape of her neck. It was so soft. They came closer, their breaths battling with each other. Their warm breath made the temperature rise. The faint smell of sandalwood was now much stronger and Lallan felt intoxicated. Any man on this earth could not have resisted such a temptation. Lallan was no Vishwamitra.

Their lips met like two cold rivers and turned into a lava-like hot spring. They melted like a scoop of ice cream over a sizzling brownie. Lallan's hand slipped from her neck to the zip of her grey jacket. He didn't take a second to slide it down. He had to deal with another layer of clothing, a T-shirt. He touched her breasts—so supple were the breasts. He feared as if he was an untouchable, touching the statue of a goddess in a Brahmin temple.

Sweety sucked his ear lobe. It was pleasure beyond words. Lallan was immersed by Sweety's forwardness. He touched Sweety's joint eyebrows and then his finger ran down her beautiful nose slipping down to her lips, which looked like petals to him, and finally resting on the cleft of her chin. They kissed again. Lallan was a bit unnerved now. They kissed for a minute. They both looked at each other to be sure of what they were getting into.

'Inexperienced?' asked Sweety in her mushy voice.

Lallan had no words to say. He was intimidated.

'I've had seven boyfriends,' Sweety whispered.

She knew how to intimidate him further. Ghonchu's reflection in the rear-view mirror was getting closer. Lallan's heart was throbbing like it would come out any moment. Yes he was naive in love.

'9769797555 is my number,' Sweety whispered and took a sharp U-turn.

Ghonchu was closer now, panting and dragging himself. Both of them were seated firmly like nothing had ever happened before.

'Get another number in someone else's name. Preferably a girl's. Call me at night,' Sweety instructed Lallan.

Lallan could not act or react. A chemical reaction stirred his whole body which made him feel paralysed. Sweety was unapologetic about everything. Not even an ounce of guilt or fear.

The car raced and Sweety braked as Ghonchu stood ahead. She got down in anger.

'You can't even guard me. You are of no use!'

'I waved you to stop,' Ghonchu clarified.

'Get your Jeep repaired or sell it off to an old garage.' Sweety started walking away in a state of haughtiness and temper. Ghonchu followed her.

Lallan stood amused by this lightning bolt of love that had struck him squarely and blinded him. He muttered her phone number like a silent chant.

18

'Thank god, we have posters of you put up all around, Minister saheb. Otherwise, I would have not have been able to recollect your face,' Radhey Shyam Yadav's sarcasm was definitely much heavier than what has a healthy dose of light humour. His lopsided smile spread half an inch longer.

Kaali Pandey had come to meet with his old friend–turned–arch rival Yadav after a good many years. Their armed bodyguards were clueless about this heavily guarded, urgent and confidential meeting between these two titans at a ramshackle farmhouse. The farmhouse was Radhey Shyam's ancestral property.

Once it used to be outside the city but gradually the city walked up to the farmhouse and made it a part of its hustle and bustle. Yadav often used this farmhouse as a marriage pandal.

'So, how much money are you making from the marriage hall every day?' asked Kaali.

'Not as much as you are. I was a foolish guy. I got happy with the breadcrumbs and you walked away with the whole cake!' Radhey Shyam replied.

No one could hear any voice coming out of the closed-door meeting. Ghonchu and battalion were waiting outside. It was all very hush-hush.

'Do you still eat Chyawanprash every morning?' Radhey Shyam Yadav tried to be pally with Kaali Pandey.

'Was it important to meet you today?' Minister saheb refused to get emotional.

'Do you remember Vidya Sukul? Oh, what a beauty! We both were after her in college,' Radhey Shyam joked.

'I have not come here to talk about our college affairs.' Kaali did not want to indulge in any kind of private banter.

'I have not become a professional like you. You are a three-term minister. I am a poor criminal who remained a daku, and could not turn into a Valmiki like you.' Radhey Shyam's sarcasm was not lost on Kaali.

'Withdraw your wife's nomination!' ordered Kaali.

'No, bhaiji. That is done. We can't step back,' Radhey Shyam replied firmly.

His wife Madhuri Yadav brought them a glass of jaljeera each. Madhuri Yadav was in a synthetic printed sari with the pallu covering her head.

'Namaste, bhaiyya,' Madhuri murmured.

Kaali Pandey did not like to look a woman in the eye. He did not acknowledge Madhuri's presence. She offered the drink to Kaali.

'We are not enemies. Please have this. The lemons are from our kitchen garden. This time there's been a good produce. Please take some for your home too . . .' She tried to be sweet.

'Bhabhiji, you are a lady. Don't jump into politics.' Kaali Pandey was direct and curt.

'We have ordered cotton saris from Khadi Bhandar for the campaigning. I have memorized the speech too.' Madhuri kept the glass on the table as Kaali refused to accept it. She sat opposite him, next to her husband.

'Try chopping vegetables, Bhabhiji, not my votes.' Kaali Pandey looked directly at Radhey Shyam, avoiding the lady.

'Get up. You must leave, if you have come to insult us.' Yadav tried getting up from his seat.

'We have been enemies for eighteen years now. Everyone knows that I have come to an enemy's place to negotiate and not retaliate,' Kaali talked like a mediator.

'Your tone is of retaliation, not negotiation,' Radhey Shyam had a razor-sharp tongue.

'So what will it take?' asked Kaali Pandey.

'We will not withdraw our nomination at any cost.'

'Really? Let me throw a blank cheque at your face!'

'To hell with money. We are contesting for prestige. You can't dominate us with your caste power any more!' Yadav snapped.

'What will it take to buy your prestige?' asked Kaali Pandey. He wanted Madhuri to withdraw her nomination at any cost.

'Marriage,' Radhey Shyam ordered shamelessly.

Madhuri looked nervous. She knew that the matchstick of conflict had just been struck. It was sure to lead to a massive inferno.

'We can talk later . . . You people can think again,' Madhuri insisted. She was trying to put a lid on a volcano.

'Get your daughter married to my son. My son could be your successor.' Radhey Shyam had his pitch ready.

Kaali Pandey got up and went closer to him. They looked at each other for a second. Then Kaali took his shoe off and slapped Radhey Shyam with it.

'You low caste! My foot. How dare you!' Kaali Pandey's blood pressure shot up. His eyes were fiery red.

Radhey Shyam held Kaali by his collar. 'Low caste?! I will rule over you Pandey . . . I was not born to be your slave like the others!' Radhey Shyam was equally hot with rage.

Hearing the loud voices, Ghonchu and other guards rushed in. The air was tense inside the room. The tension of ego, caste and politics was suffocating. The minister's armed bodyguards took only a second to point their guns at Radhey Shyam. There was pin-drop silence. The Yadavs were in shock. Everyone witnessed the beads of perspiration dotting their foreheads. They were sweating profusely.

By now Radhey Shyam had realized that he had rubbed Minister Pandey in quite a wrong way by yanking at his most sensitive nerve. Just the ghost of any mischief and Pandey's henchmen could pull the trigger. He had completely forgotten the saying he had read somewhere: a ballot is mightier than a bullet. What he wanted now was an Enfield Bullet to vanish from the scene in a jiffy.

Caste was a unique pivot around which the politics in this part of the badlands revolved. Kaali Pandey was a Brahmin who believed he was superior to the rest by virtue of his birth in this community. He could never tolerate the very idea proposed to him by Radhey Shyam as the Yadavs were predominantly a backward community. An arranged marriage between the children of these two communities was beyond social imagination. The rigidity of the caste system was further spiked by a feudal system.

Kaali Pandey stormed out. The meeting had been nothing but a pointless exchange of irrevocable insults. His armed battalion followed, while Radhey Shyam and his wife stood shell-shocked. They became normal only after the noise of the last vehicle of the minister's cavalcade disappeared. This sham of a meeting had been a matter of utter disrespect for them, their community, their aims and ambitions.

19

Lallan was on his Bullet, ready for college. He looked cheerful and boyish today. A neat shave had brought out the glee on his face.

His bike was parked outside Meetu's house. She came out running in a yellow salwar kameez. Lallan didn't like her wearing the colour. He thought that the colour was reserved for a beauty like Sweety.

Meetu opened the squeaky, iron gate. She scanned Lallan from top to toe, like some fashion robot.

'Hmm.' She wanted to say something beyond simple words.

'Thanks,' said Lallan.

'You have finished your early-morning quota of shaving?' mocked Meetu.

'I want to take you out for masala dosa.' Lallan changed the topic of their conversation.

He always switched topics if he started to feel awkward, especially when he was with Meetu.

'Yesterday it was chhola bhatura; today masala dosa! It is difficult for me to believe.' Meetu was trying to figure out the reason behind Lallan's sudden over-generosity over the last few days.

'I mean, it's okay if you don't want to . . .' said Lallan kick-starting his Bullet.

'Wait! I will come. But . . .' Meetu had a problem. She looked around. 'Actually . . . I can't come on the bike.'

'You are always after me. Everyone in this mohalla knows this, baba!' Lallan laughed at Meetu's acting like a coy girl.

'No. Nothing like that but . . .' Meetu hesitated.

'What?' Lallan looked at her.

'Wrong day of the month,' she whispered.

'Auto? Will an auto do?' Lallan was ready to negotiate for anything to be with her at that moment. He had his reasons.

'Yeah, a rickshaw will do,' Meetu smiled gratefully.

'Let me park my bike in the backyard then. Meanwhile, you hail a rickshaw,' Lallan softly instructed Meetu.

It took them exactly twenty-eight minutes to reach Basant Vihar on Fraser Road. Basant Vihar was a popular Patna hangout for upmarket young couples. It had the most effective air conditioners. Besides, they served unlimited saunf properly laced with chaman bahaar for free after the meals. Another important reason for choosing this place was that Basant Vihar was located at quite a distance from their houses. They were sitting across each other and the breeze of the AC was cooling off the hot air around them.

'I told you something very private today,' Meetu said, fiddling with the cutlery.

'That's okay.' Lallan smiled as he passed the menu to her.

'You know, it's you, only you. I know that we will get married. Otherwise, I don't discuss my private stuff with any Raju Taraju.' Raju Taraju was Meetu's self-invented vocabulary for the phrase 'Tom, Dick and Harry'.

'Plain paper dosa. I will have that.' Lallan was clear about his choice. Plain paper dosa attracts some major attention when served because of its size and Lallan somehow loved that attention.

'Rawa masala dosa with cheese,' ordered Meetu.

It took some time for their dosas to arrive. Lallan took some pickle and vinegar-soaked onion and nibbled on it.

'I can't even have achaar,' Meetu reinstated.

Lallan was somehow annoyed listening to her list of Dos and Don'ts during the 'wrong days'.

'So, exams are over. We will soon have an MBA degree. What have you decided?' Lallan changed the topic once again. He wanted to avoid any ultra-private conversation with Meetu, at any cost.

'We will find a job for you and then get married and live here.' Meetu was happy and clear.

'Job for me? And for you?' Lallan asked her.

'I am happy to live as a housewife. I don't mind knitting sweaters for you!' Meetu teased him.

'Then why did you take up an MBA course?' Lallan questioned her.

'To be with you.'

'Wow! You are something! You have no dreams . . . seriously!' Lallan looked at Meetu's triangular face. It was so different from Sweety's round face.

'I have! And it's to get married to you. Who says that is not a dream?'

The dosas arrived—a Superman-sized plain paper dosa and a rawa masala dosa.

The waiter poured sambar into Lallan's bowl. He tried ladling sambar into Meetu's bowl. He stretched to do so, as Meetu was on the other side.

It was a table for four. Lallan deliberately tried pushing one of the chairs. The waiter lost his balance and south Indian food rained all over Meetu and her plate. Her yellow salwar kameez was now splattered with sambar.

'Can't you see properly?' Meetu screamed at the waiter.

She rushed to the washroom. The waiter was hyperventilating. A junior waiter took over the cleaning. Lallan was now alone. He knew it would take a long time for Meetu to clean the salwar kameez. Lallan opened her bag in a hurry. He was shaking inside but posed calmly outside. He took out her purse and did a quick check. He flipped through the card holders and took out her voter's ID card. He sneaked it into his pocket and kept the purse back inside the bag.

The table had been rearranged. A different waiter was there to look after them. Lallan sat there calmly, as if nothing had happened. He saw Meetu coming out of the washroom.

'It is done. I am not hungry any more!' she grumbled, coming near the table.

'Come on, we have hours to spend. Don't spoil the mood. Sit.' Lallan wanted to eat the appetizing dosa. Lallan concentrated on the dosa. It was a delight to finish it from one end to the other. He lovingly took some masala aloo from Meetu's dosa to spice things up.

Meetu watched him in delight. She still wondered about Lallan's sudden interest in her.

'Ras malai?' asked Lallan to Meetu.

'No. I am full.' Meetu wanted to go home and change.

'You take a rickshaw. I have some important work.'

'What?' Meetu was shocked.

'You are still not my wife. Don't keep asking me ten thousand questions!' Lallan reminded Meetu with a sweet smile.

Meetu got up in annoyance. 'God, you are unpredictable!' She took her bag to leave.

'Don't bear with me,' Lallan teased her.

'I am not dying to marry you. I will create an account on shaadi.com!' she warned

'Don't upload your real pictures!'

Meetu looked at him angrily and stormed out. The young waiter came with the menu again.

'Ras malai . . . chilled!' ordered Lallan with pride.

20

It was a pitch-dark night. The moon was lost in the clouds. Sweety was still drenched from her recent bath, draped in her lilac bathrobe. She had a habit of getting into the cosy blanket after a bath. She took out her phone from under her pillow to read the message she had received an hour back.

This is my new number.

She called on the number. Lallan picked up the phone with a tiny whisper of 'hello'.

'Lallan! So you are not a Lally,' smiled Sweety.

'Meetu,' whispered Lallan.

'Meetu?'

'This phone is in Meetu's name,' Lallan clarified.

'And Meetu is?' Sweety asked with raised eyebrows.

'My neighbour. She has no idea that I have got this number in her name.' Lallan cleared his throat.

'We are safe!' Sweety was playing with fire. She knew it but she had always wanted to do that.

'I feel you haven't told me what you really think of me,' said Lallan.

'Did it bother you?' asked Sweety.

'Yes, it did! I couldn't wait. You created a kind of suspense!' Lallan knew that he had no right to complain. But he knew for sure that he was behaving very non-Lallan-like, for some time now and he loved it.

'Hmm . . . Firstly, how do I know that you are a Leo?' Sweety rolled her tongue like a *firangi* as she pronounced 'Leo'.

'I was wondering . . .' Lallan asked in anticipation.

'Saumi, my best friend told me,' Sweety responded proudly.

'Saumi?'

'Saumya Gupta, daughter of B.B. Gupta, is my friend. I asked her to find out more about you,' Sweety said fiddling with her wet locks.

'Then you must have also known the number of times I have failed!' Lallan wailed in a disappointed tone.

'Does it matter?' asked Sweety to boost up the man.

'The second thing?' Lallan was inquisitive.

This is the sinful pleasure of being a voyeur. Nothing which is straight and simple fascinates people who are complicated.

'Hmm.' Sweety was trying to fill in the pauses. She was actually buying time.

'What hmm? What is it?' Lallan insisted.

His heart pounded whenever he heard Sweety's 'hmm'. It was so intoxicating, like a flowing river of whiskey.

'You have never kissed anyone before! That's the second thing I wanted to tell you.'

'I . . . I was a bad kisser?'

'You were,' Sweety said and paused. 'But I'd like to train a bad kisser!'

'I have been kissing your father's arse for ages; nothing else.' Lallan was not happy to hear his report card on kissing. He felt hopeless and a little worthless—a feeling that came frequently to Lallan.

'And the third thing!' Sweety guessed the sad little boy in Lallan.

'Can you tease less?' Lallan requested.

'Oh . . . the third thing is not about your kiss or your birth sign. So relax! It's about your passion!' Sweety was excellent at pre-selling things. She made every little detail sound enticing enough to bait Lallan.

'What's my passion?' Lallan got confused. His dreams were private!

'Your business idea!' Sweety sounded as though she knew about Lallan's dream more than him.

'What do you know about it?' Lallan got curious.

'It's my promise. I will get your business idea kick-started! Sweety's promise!' She sounded surer than Kaali Pandey.

'How? How much do you know about it?'

'I will ask Papa. He will invest in your business,' Sweety announced confidently.

'He will kill both you and me!' Lallan always had his head bent in fear of Kaali Pandey. How would *he* fund his business?

'I know how to convince him!' Sweety assured Lallan. 'And you know that only I know how to convince him.' Sweety had made up her mind.

'I think we should not talk to each other,' Lallan retorted.

'Don't be a chicken! Your dream is like a Leo. In that case your approach to reach your dream should also be fearless. Just count on me. Do what I say,' Sweety pacified Lallan.

'So . . .' Lallan was totally confused. He had no clue where was he going, almost like a headless chicken.

'So, three days to go. I will convince papa to meet you and listen to your business plan.' Sweety tried calming down Lallan.

'I am not just nervous, but something more than that. We might never meet again,' Lallan warned Sweety.

'I need that kiss again!' Sweety whispered deep into her mouthpiece.

Lallan was going through a metamorphosis. He was transforming into a butterfly from a caterpillar, or perhaps vice versa; was that even possible? And it was all so terrifyingly confusing for him.

Sweety was no Meetu. He could not toy around with her. He knew that she was the only, beautiful, dangerous daughter of the most hated man within a thousand miles.

'So see you straight after three days, 11 a.m. at my home, Lallan Jha!' Sweety was ready to say her goodbye.

'No! You're rushing,' Lallan tried to stop her.

'If you are a chicken then stay in your *tokri*, enter the jungle only if you are a lion.' Sweety poked at him to take the risk.

Sweety pressed a gentle kiss on the phone.

Lallan's romance fizzled out.

Loving Sweety wasn't that easy!

21

Kaali Pandey sat like an emperor, gobbling down his greasy breakfast.

Sweety was sitting next to him. She was slowly munching on her toast.

'How is it going?' Kaali Pandey asked her.

'What?' Sweety looked lost.

'Driving,' Kaali clarified.

'Good,' Sweety took a bigger bite.

'I will be looking for some guys. I think you should get married . . .' Kaali hesitatingly told Sweety.

Sweety's reaction would have been otherwise but she controlled herself. She kept nibbling at her bread.

'Why don't you eat a fruit? It will help your health,' Sweety reminded him. 'Are you okay?' she asked him.

'Yeah, just worried. Got to know that Radhey Shyam Yadav has nominated his wife for the election.'

Sweety had a look of disgust. Yadav's name was like poison in the Pandey household. Sweety had lost her mother because of him. He was the one who kidnapped and killed her mother's brother, Suren Mama. Sweety's mother could not bear the loss and committed suicide. How could a little girl forget this?

'His feet have outgrown his shoes. I will chop them off!' Kaali Pandey growled in anger.

'You have a strong foothold. You will win!' Sweety looked at her father, finishing the last edge of the bread.

Kaali Pandey was overwhelmed to see his daughter talk sweetly with him. Generally she always spoke to him with a dash of sarcasm which left him hanging low with guilt.

He took an apple from the table and took a bite happily.

'The driver, that guy . . . Lallan?' Sweety started.

'Was he rude?' Kaali became alert.

'No. Gentle, simple guy, he is,' said Sweety.

'So?' Kaali was inquisitive.

'He has a business plan . . .' Sweety pretended to be very casual about it.

Kaali Pandey's hawk-like eyes zoomed in to scrutinize minutely what diabolical thing Sweety had in store next.

'He just told me . . . I mean while giving driving lessons,' Sweety kept pretending to be super easy and casual about it.

'What is it? He has never spoken in front of me,' said Kaali.

'You know, like everyone, he is scared but I thought that it was a good business idea and you should listen to him once. Not a bad idea to invest in.'

'I have the elections on my mind and he is running around with the idea of setting up a business in his head!' Kaali said dismissively.

'He is standing outside on the porch; listen to his idea once!' Sweety made sure that she would not let her father go away without the meeting.

'Hmm.' He looked at Ghonchu

'He is sitting outside with the dogs. Should I call him?' Ghonchu asked.

Kaali Pandey nodded his full head with half his heart. Sweety's conjecture was unusually right. Lallan was escorted in. Kaali Pandey walked towards him and looked at him from head to toe.

Kaali was looking at Lallan in a new light. Till date, Lallan had been easy pickings for Kaali and his nefarious activities. Today, Lallan was an investment opportunity.

'Welcome Ambaniji!' Kaali Pandey mocked.

'Lallan, have you brought a presentation?' Sweety wanted to keep the agenda of this meeting serious and not turn it into an amusing pastime for her disinterested father.

Lallan took out his laptop and opened a PowerPoint slideshow—a heavily designed one.

'I don't understand computer language,' Kaali Pandey showed his lack of interest at every possible step.

Lallan, with his desi MBA sensibilities, started off his presentation.

'Sir, I will take you through my plan,' he said, trembling with fear. He looked like a salesman trying to sell an LIC policy or a vacuum cleaner.

Sweety came and sat beside Kaali Pandey. She was Lallan's only source of strength in the room.

'I want to start a business providing kidnapping insurance,' Lallan said, trying to sound confident.

Kaali Pandey was a little amused.

'In Mexico, Venezuela and some other countries in Latin America, kidnapping and risk insurance has been around for a long time,' Lallan tried to explain.

Kaali Pandey was more than amused now.

'It is also a practice in Russia and in some countries of East Europe.' Lallan was proud to have completed one full sentence without spluttering.

'You making an *ullu* out of me?' asked Kaali Pandey.

'No, sir. It's a fact. In our country, that's the type of crime with an ever-increasing percentage. From 1953 to 2006, it has increased over 47.1 per cent—' The spirit of Kotler residing inside Lallan's soul was speaking out.

'So what if someone gets the insurance done?' Kaali Pandey inquired.

'We will give coverage for risk and ransom, sir.' Lallan was now ranting out details from the logistics file. He handed over a detailed report file. 'Here are the minute details of the business. I have prepared everything,' Lallan said.

'What do you want me to do?' asked Kaali Pandey.

'Invest money, sir . . . just need a few lakhs to set up this company, the first of its kind in India,' Lallan said hopefully.

'If a donkey wants to become a beautiful slut at the cost of my money, I give a damn!'' Kaali Pandey announced.

Lallan looked scared.

'You slave! You have come here to present me your great business idea!' Kaali Pandey insulted him.

'Sir, profits are huge. In only three months, the company can break even. It's a risk but a perfect risk,' Lallan tried again to explain to him.

'Take your computer and go away. I called you to teach driving to my daughter. You started giving directions. Just pick up your computer and leave!' Kaali ordered. Then he looked at Sweety and said, 'Tomorrow onwards, we are meeting some boys for you; concentrate on the right things!'

Lallan stood speechless and helpless.

'You concentrate on elections. We have to recover money from people. A lot of work to be done. Okay, Mr Ambani?' Kaali Pandey looked at Lallan with raised eyebrows.

Lallan picked up his old HCL laptop. He could not even look Sweety in the eye. He left the living room dragging his heavy feet and a heavy heart. Sweety stood, watching him go away.

Was it a full stop?

No, hopefully just a comma!

22

A sleepless night it was, again.

Lallan was on his terrace. He wanted to sleep under the sky, gazing and asking the thousands of questions, answers to which evaded him. He kept wondering whether the axe fell on the tree or the damned tree fell on the axe. How had he fallen for Sweety? Why did he listen to her instructions of presenting his plan in front of the demon who had mocked and crushed it? He felt like a slave once again!

He was lying on his charpoy with a thin *chaddar* draped over him—a cream one that barely covered him. His phone was resting on his chest. It vibrated.

'S' calling, his screen informed him.

He picked up the phone reluctantly.

'Meetu,' whispered a voice.

'It's over,' said Lallan.

'It isn't that easy!' the sexy, coarse voice whispered.

'Why did we do this?' Lallan asked. His innocence showed in his voice.

'Come to my room,' Sweety invited him.

'You want to get me killed or what?' Lallan was positively furious.

'Ok, I will come to you.' Sweety sounded to be in a hurry.

'Are you mad?' Lallan warned her.

'I'm half-way there!'

'What?' Lallan looked around.

'I have to meet you. I am going to Saumya's home. She is home for a pooja at her place,' Sweety explained.

'So? What's your plan?' Lallan knew that Sweety was trying to cook up something dangerous all over again.

'I will be escorted by Ghonchu; I will be picked up and dropped back by him, later on. Will get an hour of alone time!' she said playfully.

Everything seemed like a game to Sweety, while it was no longer so for Lallan. He knew that this wonderland of love would cost him dearly.

'Our lives are different . . . Let's not join the dots,' Lallan warned her again, this time with a heavier voice.

'Our meeting is on. Try to make it to the Gupta mansion by 10 a.m. tomorrow. I will give you a call and sneak you into Saumya's room.' Sweety's coarse voice had a huskiness which made Lallan go weak in the knees even though he knew he might lose his kneecaps for doing so.

'I am not pushing myself into this fire!' Lallan protested.

'I will pull you out! Just give me your hand!' Sweety smiled and hung up.

Lallan looked at his half-chewed nails. He always bit his nails when anxious.

He got up and looked at the thirty-seven gods and goddesses. He tried to soak in some of their radiance, but he just felt weak, numb and helpless. His heart has been skinned off. He had no control over his emotions. He wanted to stay away from Sweety but Sweety was like a beautiful witch drowning him with love.

Sweety had managed to represent both his bondage and his liberation. He was clueless which one she would ultimately turn out to be. It was a scary thought, but it excited him nonetheless.

23

10 a.m.

A white BMW arrived at Gupta Niwas. Sweety stepped out in a white Hakoba-knit kurti with a bright pink churidaar. A zip stitched into the reverse of her kurti was more than doing its job to keep her look tight in place, accentuating her curves. A white chiffon dupatta with tiny pink woollen balls bobbing around on the edge completed the look.

Sweety wore silver Kolhapuri chappals showing off her painted bubble-gum-pink nails.

She was escorted by Ghonchu.

Satyanarayan Katha was resonating through the mansion as Sweety stepped in with her sandalwood aroma.

Earthen diyas fuelled by pure ghee had been placed all around, adding a warm and colourful glow to the proceedings. Saumya was seated beside her father. Sweety waved at Saumya.

Sweety left her slippers at the entrance, as a mark of respect and went in to sit beside Saumya. Ghonchu knew well enough to mind his own business and walked out.

Satyanarayan Katha is quite an interesting ritual practised in India. It's a very popular ritual in most parts of India, including Karnataka, Andhra Pradesh, Gujarat, West Bengal, Orissa, Maharashtra and parts of North India. The exact origins of this popular pooja are not known for certain.

The pooja consists of worshipping to Satyanarayan, an extremely benevolent avatar of Vishnu.

Saumya's brother was sitting for the pooja as it was his first day of business.

Saumya and her brother were like chalk and cheese. He was unattractive like a tadpole, had a little paunch that made him look three months pregnant. He had a squeaky voice, as if he was still stuck in adolescence even though he was actually twenty-one.

He was pursuing an MBA from his father's institute and was a classmate of Lallan. Mr Gupta had opened the third sanitary store with a range of Italian bathtubs and commodes. He had dedicated this venture to his highly incapable son, Bikram.

In Bihar, 'v' becomes 'b' and 's' becomes 'sh' at its own convenience.

Vikram became Bikram not because of some fancy astrology intervention but because of the phonetic incapability of Mr Gupta and his family.

Bikram had always liked Sweety but was too scared to even compliment her. He smiled at her hesitantly. Sweety smiled back.

'Today you will be tested!' Sweety whispered in Saumya's ears.

'Not really in the mood today. I did not sleep at all last night; I had to come by train.' Saumya surrendered though, even before finding out what Sweety had in store for her.

'Your room is upstairs,' Sweety told her knowingly.

'What do you mean?' Saumya was busy offering milk, flower petals and coins to the deity.

'I am smuggling someone into your room in the next twenty minutes,' Sweety announced in a whisper.

Saumya stopped. She looked at her in shock. Saumya had a pot full of milk in her hand. Realizing that all eyes were on her, she quickly passed it on to the lady next to her as the pot was passing hands with every line of the Katha being read.

'Are you nuts?' Saumya asked her mad friend.

She noticed her father staring at them whispering. By then, the pot of milk had come a full circle. The old lady next to Sweety passed it to her. Sweety got a chance. She let the pot slip out of her hands and her white kurti got drenched.

It was worth it to get the attention.

'Saumya, give me a kurti to change into,' Sweety said and dragged her friend away from the pooja.

'You are inviting trouble, Sweety, and I am not going to play along,' Saumya warned Sweety as they took the stairs to her room.

'I have called him here. He will be there in ten minutes. He will come through the backdoor.' Sweety knew every nook and cranny of Saumya's house from a childhood playing hide-and-seek there.

'Who is this "he"?' Saumya looked utterly confused.

'You know,' Sweety smiled.

'Driving master?' Saumya rolled her eyes.

'That's why you are my best friend, yes!'

'I am not letting this happen!'

Sweety's phone rang—a missed call.

'I think he is here,' Sweety looked out of the window.

Saumya's heart leapt into her mouth and her brain stopped functioning.

Lallan was there, wearing a white shirt.

'Don't let him climb the pipe like in the movies!' Saumya warned. She knew that she could not thwart this tsunami of stolen love. So, the best idea was to go along with it.

'Come on. The storeroom gate opens directly into the courtyard where he is standing. Sneak him in and send him up by the spiral staircase to the first floor,' Sweety directed Saumya as if it was her own home. 'And don't panic! The keys are on top of the fridge in the blue tin box.'

'I will never forgive you for this!' Saumya muttered as she left the room, almost trembling out of fear.

Sweety looked relaxed and calm as she flounced on Saumya's bed.

She plugged in her earphones and listened to her favourite number 'Baahon ke darmiyaan' on her phone. The spreading island of milk on her white kurti was slowly drenching her.

In a while, Lallan came into the room, led by Saumya.

'Ten minutes. I am waiting outside the door. He has to be out or I will be dead!' said Saumya. She stepped out, locked the door and stood there like a guard.

Lallan and Sweety were there, alone in a room for the first time. The ten-minute countdown was playing on their minds. Sweety got up and walked to him.

Lallan looked terrified. Sweety took the remote control kept beside the bed and switched on the TV. A random food show flashed on, showing an attractive cook who was trying to make spinach and okra stir fry. Lallan turned at the suddenly loud TV.

'Spinach means *palak*, okra means *bhindi*, stir fry means fried in less oil. It's all the magic of words,' Sweety had the composure of a calm sea—unpredictable.

She was beyond Lallan's comprehension.

'This is our last meeting. Things will never happen between us,' Lallan said shakily.

'What if Dad said no! I can get money for your business,' Sweety went up to Lallan and held his hand.

Lallan melted in Sweety's hands. His soul sang. 'Your help will cost us our lives . . .' he tried to explain.

'I have a plan. How much do you need for your business? One crore? We can get it now!' Sweety had a conjuring magician's confidence sparkling in her almond eyes.

'How?' Lallan's eyes bore into Sweety's. He wanted to know whether all this was a bout of insanity, love or devilish devastation.

'We could kidnap Saumya, right now!' Sweety whispered with a smile.

'What?' Lallan covered Sweety's errant mouth with a shaking palm. He knew that one more word from Sweety's mouth could get him into trouble.

Sweety tried pushing him away.

'I have everything that you would need in my bag—chloroform, Saumya's car keys, some cash. You take her from her home, like a proxy kidnapping, and get some ransom. Then, you drop her back and you'll have gotten your seed money.'

Lallan was left speechless.

'Gupta uncle has lots of money for that dumb brother of Saumya's. He is opening a new store—Italian bathtubs and Jacuzzis. I have heard one bathtub costs lakhs. Uncle will instantly shell out money to save Saumya. No one will know that it's you, no one has seen you coming into the house,' Sweety said confidently.

'Saumya knows all about this ridiculous idea of yours?' Lallan asked Sweety.

'No.'

'You got me wrong! I am crazy about my dream, but not this crazy. You planned to kidnap your friend to fund my dreams? And she doesn't even know. She is guarding us!' Lallan moved towards the door looking as if he simply wanted to disappear.

Sweety held his hand to stop him. Lallan turned around.

'So, where is my goodbye kiss?' Sweety said, her eyes glistening with tears.

Lallan was totally wrought by this mischievous, magical, ridiculous young lady standing in front of him.

'We might never meet again, I guess.' Tears rolled down Sweety's face.

Lallan went and hugged her. Her tears soaked his white shirt.

For a moment, the world just stopped. This was probably the first and the last hug where their bosoms met shyly like sky and earth. Both had so many unspoken and unknown feelings filling up their hearts that it was an overbearing moment.

Suddenly the conch rang out, loud and clear. The Satyanarayan Pooja would end soon and the aarti would commence. The door opened.

'Enough. Ten minutes are up,' Saumya said.

Lallan and Sweety stood looking at each other. This painful feeling of love had turned them to stone.

'This stupid game is over. Let's run, the pooja is ending and the aarti will begin,' Saumya warned.

Sweety kissed him again on his dry lips as if it was the last stamp before the post made its way for a foreign destination.

Lallan faded away in front of Sweety's eyes. Saumya shooed him out like a whirlwind, taking him down the spiral stairs in the corner to the storeroom.

Sweety looked out of the window. She saw her man walking away.

24

Kaali Pandey's shoes were always black and shiny, as if even the dust was scared enough to stay away from him.

Ghonchu helped Kaali take off his shoes. He was back from his election meetings and propaganda settings. The filing of election nominations was three days away. In Patna, every single atom gets charged with election mania.

Ghonchu pulled off the socks gently and tucked them inside the shoes.

'Sweety?' asked Kaali.

'She went for pooja at Saumya's home earlier. She is resting in her room now.'

'Lallan seems to be completely jobless. Order him to collect *wasooli*s from our list of Lalas,' Kaali ordered.

Ghonchu took out Moov gel from his denim jeans' rear pocket. The application of this gel was part of his KRA.

He gently rubbed the gel on Kaali's chapped foot.

'Aaaaah.' A long sigh escaped the demon's mouth.

Kaali extracted his gold tooth cap and took it out on his palm.

'Get it polished.' Kaali handed it over carefully to Ghonchu. He took it with his left hand and kept it wrapped in a handkerchief.

Sweety came downstairs with her guitar.

Ghonchu was an expert in melting into the background when Sweety was with Kaali Pandey. He knew that these brief interactions between father and daughter always ended in painful blasts of anger and insulting verbal volleys.

'Are you having lunch with me?' Kaali asked, adjusting himself on the couch. The couch had a depression right in the middle, into which Kaali Pandey sank his ample girth every day.

'I am not hungry. I had enough at Gupta Uncle's.' Sweety looked for a magazine, shuffling the newspaper stack.

'Bikram is a nice guy and now even settled.' Kaali Pandey tried to gauge Sweety's interest. She kept looking for her magazine.

'I don't know who mixes my magazines with the newspapers,' Sweety grumbled.

'You have to get married. Saumya is your friend. The Guptas are moneyed and we know each other well.'

Though the Guptas belonged to a lower caste, bank statements scored over caste certificates.

'You focus on your elections, let me focus on my boring life,' Sweety replied.

'Your only intention is to make me feel guilty,' Kaali complained.

'Like my mother, you will lose me one day too! I will die of this loneliness!' Sweety howled.

The smell of the Moov gel had strongly taken over the atmosphere of the drawing room, where the father and daughter duo sat sullenly glaring at each other.

'That's why I want you to get married,' Kaali insisted.

'To divert me?' Sweety shrieked.

'To engage you,' Kaali retorted.

'I wanted to be a pop singer, a diva, a queen!' Sweety glared at her father.

'You are my princess!' Kaali tried to calm her down

'I am just a remote-controlled toy in your hand,' Sweety said, revolted.

'Elections are dangerous. Anything can happen. I can't let you roam free. You might be at risk,' Kaali tried to pacify his angry tigress.

'So, for your dreams, your victory, I have to sacrifice my happiness just as my mother ended up doing!' Sweety had a spiteful look in her eyes. Her eyes were red and filmed with unshed tears.

Ghonchu dared to intervene in this tough emotional war between father and daughter.

'Sir, some *kaand* happening,' Ghonchu announced.

Kaali Pandey looked at him confused.

'Radhey Shyam Yadav wants to meet you privately today, at 2 p.m. sharp, before filing the nomination.'

Kaali Pandey looked relieved. He had a feeling that he would have ended up surrendering to his reckless daughter. Even fate had surrendered earlier in front of Kaali.

Sweety looked at her father with her overburdened eyes. 'You know how to win!' Sweety screamed with sarcasm and stomped off to her room.

25

Radhey Shyam Yadav welcomed Kaali Pandey with folded hands.

Kaali Pandey was practically grinning.

'I want to surrender,' Yadav said, with his hands still folded.

Kaali seated himself more comfortably on the sofa.

'Can't even offer water as it would be insulting for you to accept a lower caste man's offering,' Yadav sounded humble and contained.

'I am so glad you decided to take back the nomination. Why get your woman to contest against me?' Kaali was happy with this sudden change of heart.

'Eighteen years ago, bhaiji . . . You know what happened,' Yadav reminded him.

'It was eighteen years ago.' Pandey wanted to skip the discussion.

'You know, nowadays, so many MMS clips are made. Those years, only VCR was there.'

He switched on the VCR and TV.

'Remember? We used to have video cassettes—for our marriage, kids' birthdays. Let's relive those moments. You did not come for my son's birthday, right?' Yadav pressed play on the VCR.

Kaali Pandey was stumped.

A video of children singing happy birthday started playing. Blurry, sepia-shade footage.

'What are you trying to say?' Kaali Pandey looked uncomfortable.

'I was absent on my son's third birthday. You know where I was?' Yadav quizzed the uncomfortable Pandey.

Kaali Pandey got up with a start.

'I have enough to do. I didn't come here for all this melodrama. Why don't you just get to the point?' Kaali was angry.

'The video will tell you everything.' Yadav fast-forwarded the footage and paused as the frame zoomed in on Kaali Pandey.

A much younger Kaali Pandey with a young Radhey Shyam Yadav in a closed room.

'Don't panic. It's the same room, just that we had no sofas, no chandeliers then. Now we have them,' Yadav said with a wry smile.

He played the video as Kaali sat stunned. There he was, eighteen years ago, ordering the kidnapping and killing of his own brother-in-law, Suraj, so that he could garner sympathy from people to bring in votes. Besides, his death would fetch Kaali Pandey a lot of property as he was the only sibling of Kaali's wife.

The dreaded mafia kingpin had dreamt of entering politics and this was his first dirty move. And it had worked, leading to a sympathy wave among the voting public.

Kaali Pandey was sweating as if he had been stuffed into a sauna.

'Your daughter doesn't know that her mother committed suicide because she got to know the truth,' Yadav said. 'I had kept it a secret, all these years, but not any more!'

'Don't do this!' Kaali Pandey shouted.

'No, not like this. I want the Brahmin to fall at my feet, the feet of this soiled lower caste man, and beg!'

'I would rather die!' Kaali Pandey's ego spoke out loud and clear.

'No, I will not let you die. You will have to live with it!' Yadav laughed.

'Don't trick me,' Kaali warned him.

'Marry your daughter to my son or get me thirty crores!'

'Impossible!'

'Then stand by for this video to first reach your daughter and then the whole country. It's the Internet era now. One click and your cupboard full of skeleton goes viral!' Yadav laughed again.

'I will try and get the money, give me a month,' replied a broken Kaali Pandey.

'You have fifteen days. Just fifteen days. Oh, all right, make it sixteen! For old times' sake.'

Kaali Pandey left cursing his tortured and devilish soul for his past sins that were now catching up with him.

It would disrobe him in public, this dirty naked piece of truth.

26

Sweety knew only half the story. She could sense the pall of doom gripping the mansion. She knew that her father was hanging between the cliffs of Death vs Defeat.

Sweety sat beside her father who had not eaten a morsel for the past two days.

Kaali was sitting alone under a bleak night bulb, surrounded by a pile of files.

'You have to arrange for the money?' asked Sweety.

Kaali Pandey gave a dull nod.

'Can I help?' asked Sweety

'Just hug me,' Kaali Pandey had almost pleaded.

Sweety hugged him without any warmth and a great deal of awkwardness.

'Yadav is negotiating?' asked Sweety.

'Thirty crores.'

'For withdrawing nominations?'

'Hmm and much more. Something which would dent my life.'

'You have to pay for your crimes someday.' Sweety distanced herself.

'For the first time, I want to die.' Kaali had tears streaming down his eyes.

Sweety observed her father crying for the first time in his life.

'Is it guilt or fear?' asked Sweety.

'Both.'

'How will you arrange for thirty crores?'

'Looks impossible and I have tried everything. Still short of ten crores.'

'It is possible.' Sweety looked deep into her father's eyes.

Kaali Pandey did not look very convinced. His beautiful daughter jumped the gun and came up with the weirdest ideas most of the time.

'Lallan can do it!' said Sweety.

Kaali was more amused now.

'His business idea can fetch you ten crores in fifteen days.'

Kaali was trying to put the twos together but it was not adding up to a four.

'Kidnapping insurance!' exclaimed Sweety.

'HOW?'

'You start up his business and insure me as a client. I will execute my own kidnapping. You recover the ransom of ten crores from the insurance,' explained Sweety.

It seemed that Philip Kotler's *aatma* had transferred into Sweety's body. She sounded like a strategist. She was narrating the script of a thriller.

The next fortnight of her life was about to become a spine-chilling thriller. Lallan and Sweety were going to script a kidnapping. Kaali Pandey had no choice, absolutely no choice but to play a role.

27

Lallan liked to sleep on the terrace. The cot was covered by a mosquito net. He lay inside. He could not chase away memories of Sweety's touch, her aroma, her supple breasts, her wet lips and soft palms. He tossed and turned. He wanted to omit a few chapters of his life but would forgetting Sweety be that easy? He saw the stars high in the sky. He knew that he could only gaze at them and never touch them. Sweety was like these twinkling stars.

While he was lost in joining the dots of the stars, a tiny face popped up and blocked his view.

'Dhappa,' said the face! It was Meetu, of course.

'You didn't tell me that you are sleeping on the terrace today;' Meetu whispered.

'Go home, please. I want to be alone.' Lallan was curt.

She slipped her hand inside the net and touched his chest. He cringed.

'You scared of me?' asked Meetu. She slipped inside the net. Lallan got scared and withdrew under his sheet.

'You are imagining something, na?' Meetu looked deep into his eyes.

'Buzz off!'

'How long would I keep buzzing off?' Meetu tried to pull him closer.

'Meetu!' Lallan tried stopping her.

'Kiss me once . . . you will feel love . . .' Meetu pulled him closer to her.

Lallan wanted to shout, Meetu covered his mouth.

She gave him a wet kiss in the middle of his chest.

Lallan wanted to stop all this.

She pushed him down to the pillow and bent forward on his chest. Lallan felt suffocated.

'I am not going to rape you, so chill,' she said.

'You know what? I love someone else,' muttered Lallan.

Meetu stared at him. 'Liar.' Meetu was sure that Lallan had no time to love any girl. He was too engrossed in his own weird world.

'I swear on my business dream,' Lallan tried to convince her.

'Who?' Meetu asked, moving away.

'Can't tell you the name,' Lallan looked at her with pursed lips.

Meetu kissed him on his lips. His lips felt cold like wooden blocks left overnight in a garden on a wintry night.

'It's summer. You are cold?' Meetu questioned him, playfully.

'Your charms will not work.' Lallan declared like a thief.

'It will . . .' Meetu started sliding her finger down his chest.

Lallan felt dizzy and nauseated. He tried wriggling out of the mosquito net. It seemed that the net was a like a trap.

Meetu knew she was going to lose this moment too. She held him by his hand.

Lallan was too huge to be handled with force. Meetu knew that he was slipping out of her hands. In a rage of emotions, she bit him on his wrist. Lallan fumed and, instead of screaming, he slapped across her face. Meetu's eyes welled up immediately.

Lallan realized that he had been too harsh on her but this time he didn't want to apologize.

'I am not sorry for this. If you try this again, you will have it again,' Lallan said angrily.

Meetu looked steadily at his face. Lallan knew she could slap him in return. He was ready for it. He thought that nature would balance the karma and this would be forgiven.

Meetu looked at him for few seconds and then kicked him with her knees where it hurts the most. This was equally uncalled for too.

'Hisaab barabar, we're even!' Meetu announced, with burning red eyes. She stormed downstairs like a missile.

28

Night slipped into morning.

Kaali Pandey's contemplation led only to a confusing conclusion. The conclusion was confusing because he was risking his most precious possession. Planning a pretend kidnap of his own daughter gave him the shivers. He had thought that he was the king of the jungle and he alone was the lion until the previous evening but someone had blasted his notion. Yadav was nothing in front of him. But past mistakes can turn even ants into elephants. Yadav was fast becoming the wildfire that could burn down Kaali's fiefdom.

Kaali knew that it would be worse than defeat if Sweety got to know the real story. Sweety had grown to hate Kaali Pandey. She thought that her father's terror had resulted in a conflict leading to her mother's younger brother's kidnapping and murder by Radhey Shyam Yadav due to which her mother had decided to end her life. She had therefore hated every word, every touch, and even the sight of her father since then.

If the real story ever came out, Kaali Pandey's existence as a father and a politician would be burnt to ashes. Sweety would never see his face again or perhaps do something even more drastic. After all she had Kaali's genes!

Kaali's eyes looked swollen with all the stress and anxiety. He sat quietly in the balcony adjoining his room. He stared at the steaming teapot. He was lost in his conflicting thoughts.

A beautiful hand poured some tea into the cup. The rich masala tea was a morning ritual for him but it was always served by a servant.

'I think this is the first time you are sitting here,' Sweety said in a low voice.

Kaali Pandey had not sat in his balcony for several years. He looked at his daughter, surprised. He had craved for such a moment all through his life. Sweety had never shared morning tea with him. He wanted to hug her tight but knew that she would give him the cold shoulder.

'You've never seen the stars, watched the trees grow or heard birds sing.' Sweety said all this to make Kaali feel bad.

'I think I never got the time.' Kaali looked around.

'To think beyond yourself,' Sweety added.

'Your sarcasm does not bother me.'

'So, should we call Lallan post breakfast?' Sweety asked him. Her voice was perfectly balanced—no enthusiasm, no hurry and no anxiety.

'Are you sure?' Kaali looked at Sweety. He was still trying to figure out if this was the only way.

'Your wish . . . I just thought of helping you out.' Sweety rose from her seat and added, 'It depends on how important it is for you to win!' Sweety looked straight in her father's eyes like a diplomat.

'It's more than a win . . . It's blackmail,' said Kaali Pandey.

'What's the blackmail about?' Sweety enquired.

'Something to tarnish my image . . . something I would not like to discuss.' Kaali wanted to keep it short.

'And you are still short of ten crores to put a full stop to this blackmailing business?' Sweety did her mathematics.

'I have no other option. This Lallan thing . . . I don't know.' Kaali was still contemplating.

'I am sure Lallan will behave like a trembling goat. You will have to convince him,' trilled on Sweety.

'Huh, convince? I only know how to order him.' Kaali's ego jumped up again.

'We will sail through. Our boat should not sink.' Sweety sounded like the captain of a drowning ship.

'I will ask Ghonchu to send him the message.' Kaali looked a bit convinced with this half-baked idea.

Sweety had a Monalisa smile on her face.

'You will be with us?' Kaali asked her.

Sweety tilted her head, thought for a while and then shook her head.

29

Lallan had discovered a way to get rid of all his stress—washing clothes. The entrepreneur in him felt proud of doing the laundry. He had this noble thought that cleaning in any form is good for the society, at least the intent to clean the system sustains in one's heart and mind. He often used a wooden bat to beat the wet clothes. The force with which he was beating the clothes up was good enough to even wipe out the printed stripes on his shirts. He was lost in thought, perhaps about how Meetu had cut him down to his actual size, when he was interrupted.

'So, you have fallen to this level? You misbehaved with Meetu last night? I never thought that my son, son of a high-class Maithil Brahmin, would stoop to this level! Why did god not call me to him before all this?' This rapid fire of questions came from his father. They were powerful enough to compel Lallan to stop beating the clothes and look up.

'You slapped an innocent girl? How could you even do that?' Lallan's mother was in tears. She was all set to start a fresh battle in support of the women empowerment movement in India.

'Your nikammapan, laziness has made you a frustrated soul Lallan!' screamed his father. Lallan's father could never understand his son's idea of entrepreneurship. Lallan neither took any interest in his driving school nor was he ever successful in the business ideas he had been trying for long. Getting a job somewhere was also never on his list of things to do. But yes, his attitude was very much that of a young, dynamic and successful entrepreneur.

The fiery allegations of Lallan Jha's parents gradually gathered momentum and Lallan was nothing more than a punching bag. This was a case where the target is completely cornered and taken by surprise and has no choice but to face all the possible volleys coming his way.

Suddenly a very high-pitched chanting of the Gayatri mantra started in the background. It was their doorbell. His family firmly believed that the chanting of the Vedic mantras are powerful enough to purify the environment in and around their homes. The Gayatri mantra doorbell actually shifted the high-octane war in the family into silent mode though Lallan's father was still shaking in anger.

'Bade Sarkar has asked Lallan to come to his darbar immediately,' said the most uncivilized Ghonchu. He was never expected, let alone at this point of time. Lallan had to leave his grand washing programme midway to attend to the uninvited guest. Ghonchu had a flair for doing such jobs for Minister Kaali Pandey where he could get the opportunity to show off and get sadistic pleasure.

'I'm not in mood to go to your temple right now.' Lallan showed some attitude to go to Kaali Pandey's mansion. He was caught totally unaware when Ghonchu pointed a revolver at his head without any notice.

'Don't ever dare to mess around when it involves our sarkar Minister Kaali babu!' Ghonchu was serious.

Mothers in middle-class India are the best troubleshooters we have in our country. Lallan's mother was slightly more pragmatic than the ever-crying Nirupa Roy, the famous actress who played numerous middle-class crying mothers in a number of Indian films. She wasted no time in offering a glass of sherbet to Ghonchu.

'Beta, you work so hard! Have a glass of this bel sherbet; it's very good for health and mental peace,' said Lallan's mother. 'My son never drinks this and that's why he has lost all his power to take good decisions, beta. Please don't mind his words. We will send him to Minister Pandeyji's mansion in no time.'

Lallan always hated such spontaneous star performances by his mother to safeguard her son. Ghonchu put his pistol back in his pocket. He had a victorious smile on his arrogant face. Lallan's father was still shaking, but this time not with anger. Lallan had no option but to follow Ghonchu. All his dirty and wet clothes were still lying in the bucket waiting for Lallan to come back and finish his task. It was actually a rarity for Lallan's clothes to enjoy such rituals once in a while and that day's episode was rather shortlived.

30

Sweety, Lallan and Kaali were sitting in the balcony. They were sipping hot tomato soup and Kaali was making loud, slurping noises. It was as if a vacuum cleaner was suctioning the soup from the cup.

'Papa wants to invest in your business.' Sweety wanted to cut short the story.

The soup burnt the tip of Lallan's tongue at this unexpected news. He placed the soup bowl back on the table.

'Don't worry; you will not burn your fingers like your tongue.' Sweety tried to speed up the story with a little tease.

Lallan could not see eye-to-eye with Kaali Pandey. Kaali pressed a bell and a servant came running.

'Get my new Ray Ban and give it to him!' Kaali ordered.

Lallan had always found this house the weirdest thing on the planet. It was distasteful and the creatures living under the roof were unpredictable.

The servant brought a pair of sunglasses with a golden, aviator frame fitted with jet-black glass pieces.

'Wear it and look at me!' Kaali ordered Lallan.

Lallan did as instructed. He looked at Sweety as if she was the one who teased him like a mouse with a bread piece in her hand and got him here in the mousetrap. Sweety gestured to him to wear the glasses. He did so.

'Sweety convinced me to put money in your business; I will. But it will come with a cost,' Kaali Pandey looked at Lallan donning his Ray Ban.

Lallan was silently shaking like a lamb.

'You will be you . . . but you will see and do things my way . . . under my nose!' Kaali instructed.

'It's just that I will be the first person to get insured,' Sweety tried to explain the business deal.

'But there is a catch,' Kaali said.

'You will have to kidnap me. Pretend to kidnap me!' Sweety added.

Lallan took out the sunglasses nervously and got up.

'Why? Are you scared?' Kaali Pandey mocked.

'Listen. Your dream is getting fulfilled and so will be ours,' Sweety tried to convince him.

'It is not possible. What are you saying? You are asking me to dare beyond dare!' Lallan refuted.

'Nothing is beyond dare!' Sweety, as always, tried to push him past the boundaries he had created for himself.

'The thing is, we need five crores. Urgently!'

'It's like you are fixing me up . . .' Lallan stuttered.

'No fixing! You will be a winner. Let me explain how!' Sweety rolled out a chart and took out a Reynolds pen. She scribbled on the paper like a printing machine.

'The plan is pretty simple,' she began. 'Papa needs five crores to give to Radhey Shyam Yadav as he is blackmailing him. Now we need to find that money.'

'We don't need to tell him the whole story,' Kaali instructed Sweety.

'Half stories don't lead anywhere!' Sweety left the pen and got up in anger.

'Okay, beta. Don't be angry. We can't afford to fight with each other now!' Kaali cajoled his princess.

'So anyway, Papa will invest in your business today.' Sweety sounded sure and confident.

Kaali Pandey handed him a suitcase of money.

'Now you inaugurate your kidnapping insurance business and become a hero!' Sweety smiled.

'Newspapers will talk about the new entrepreneur in town who has introduced kidnapping insurance,' Kaali Pandey added. 'And I will be the first one to insure my most precious belonging—my daughter Sweety!' Kaali said and looked at him.

'And then I will be kidnapped!' Sweety sounded like Lady M.

'Who will kidnap—' Lallan began innocently.

'You!' said Kaali.

Lallan got up in shock. 'We will be jacked!' Lallan protested.

'No, we will not. The kidnapping will be a proxy one! You will have to kidnap me because we trust you and no one else. Moreover this plan should not be known to anyone other than us,' said Sweety.

'You will safely hide Sweety somewhere. We will call for the ransom. Your insurance company will get its first case. You will give the ransom money. Sweety will be freed and all of us will be happy!' Kaali made it all sound so simple as if the whole idea of kidnapping insurance had been conceptualized by him and not Lallan.

'If the police get involved and I get caught?' Lallan asked.

'No, don't worry. You are taking me safely to a place which Papa has arranged. Nepal border—350 km from here,' Sweety announced.

Lallan could not breathe.

'Take off those glasses!' ordered Sweety. 'Look up. Look me in the eye. You need to dare now!'

Lallan was in a cage with the lion and his cub. He had no way out.

'Congratulations! Your dream is coming true!' Sweety extended her hand.

Lallan's hands were ice cold.

'Ten days to go for the kidnapping!' Kaali announced with a thumbs-up to Lallan.

Lallan looked at Sweety as if he was being butchered for love. He placed the Ray Bans on the table. He surrendered.

31

Ten uneventful days had now passed them by.

Lallan's shirt was unbuttoned. He had a habit of wearing his shirt asymetrically as he always ended up putting the buttons in the wrong holes. He had a towel around his waist. His hair was wet.

'I am going to feed bananas to the black cow, Lallan. Keep a watch; the main door is open!' his mother screamed from outside the half-open door. Overwhelmed by Lallan's new business, she had vowed to feed green bananas to black cows every day for three months.

Lallan was busy trying to button his shirt properly. His door opened with a thud. It was Meetu. She always wore Indian clothes, but today she was wearing jeans and a black top that clung to her skinny frame. She had a bunch of newspapers in her hand.

Lallan got conscious and held his towel tight. 'There is something called permission!' he yelled at her. 'There is something called sharing,' she said, coming closer.

'I am busy.' Lallan nervously started to button his shirt faster, his hands trembling. Meetu threw the papers on the bed, pulled him close and started buttoning him up. 'We get to know through papers?' she asked.

'Yes. It's no big deal.' Lallan sounded distant. Meetu held him by his chin. 'It's a big deal, Lallan! You started your dream business. It must not have been easy to convince investors,' she said, trying to look into his eyes.

'Can we talk later?' Lallan pulled away.

'You have insured even the minister's daughter! That's a big deal, baba!' Meetu held him by his wrist. She suddenly seemed to have developed superhuman energy. She pushed him on to the tattered Dunlop sofa. Then she began to unzip her top.

'Are you mad?' Lallan tried to push her off. She tried to take off his towel.

'Why wait for tomorrow? Let's become one.' Lallan struggled, but she pinned him down.

She smelt the opposite of sandalwood. She smelt of neem soap.

'Yuck. You smell of neem soap,' he said, finally pushing her off.

'And you? Who do you think you are? You smell of Dettol,' Meetu retorted. She got off and zipped her top back up.

Lallan was stunned for a moment. Meetu sat down on the tattered velvet sofa and started sobbing. 'Don't start this now. Please, Meetu,' Lallan said.

'Tell me once. Why don't you like me?' Meetu asked. Lallan kept quiet.

'Am I too dark for you?' she asked.

'It doesn't matter.'

'No, I know, I am not of your shade—not to your taste,' Meetu sobbed.

'It's not like that, Meetu. I am not sure what I want from life. I just know that you love me a lot and I don't love you even a bit,' he said.

'So we will never be together?' Meetu asked.

'We won't, Meetu. I am not even attracted towards myself. How can I be attracted to anyone else? Don't take this otherwise; you are a great girl.' Lallan tried to pacify her.

'Don't give me that!' Meetu sulked and sobbed some more.

Lallan held her cold hands and tried to be warm. 'I am going for a seven-day trip to Delhi, I have some business work. I am getting late.' Lallan wanted to hurry but didn't want to make it look like he was being inconsiderate.

'Should I not waste my time on you?' Meetu asked hopefully.

'Not even a second,' Lallan answered. Speaking bluntly felt natural; it never seemed to take him any effort.

Meetu buried her face in Lallan's chest and started sobbing loudly.

'I always thought that we will belong to each other, that we will get married. Now you are settled, your business has worked out, and I thought you would pay more attention to me,' Meetu cried.

Lallan kept mum.

'It's difficult to think of a future without you. I have loved you for whatever you are. I have always loved you. How will

I marry someone else?' she sobbed. 'It's okay, Meetu. You deserve someone better than me!' Lallan cajoled her.

'I want to do something to you. My last desire . . .' Meetu looked up at him.

'What?' Lallan asked, knowing well what the answer would be. He knew that she wanted to kiss him.

'Please, Lallan . . . just one last thing!' Meetu insisted.

Lallan gave in. 'Close your eyes,' she muttered, and so he did.

Lallan was resigned to his fate. He wasn't a bad guy at heart. He felt miserable that he had always treated Meetu like a housefly, shooing her away. He didn't want to hurt her any more. He sat there composed, with his eyes closed. He felt Meetu coming closer to him. He held his breath; he could feel Meetu's face hovering over his.

She slapped him across his face.

Lallan sat there in shock, his mouth agape.

'I loved you with all my heart,' Meetu said bitterly as she left his room.

32

Sweety had almost packed her stuff in two small suitcases. She was in a black burkha. Sweety had always been inspired by Bollywood tricks—wearing burkhas to camouflage herself was one of her fantasies.

She was packing her guitar in the case when Kaali Pandey entered her room silently, watching his madcap daughter scripting a new story which scared even him. 'Are you mad? You are taking the guitar?' he asked.

'You know I can't live without it.'

'But—' Kaali was utterly confused.

'You can't carry your luggage! You are getting kidnapped today!' he tried to explain to his gypsy daughter.

'How can I leave without my clothes, my guitar and my make-up?' Sweety asked, panicking a little.

Kaali gave her a small bag with the label 'pachranga achaar'. It was covered in oil stains and had a peculiar smell of spices and sweat. 'What's this?' a revolted Sweety asked. 'Money,' Kaali whispered. Sweety gingerly took the bag from him.

'No one will suspect that it is loaded with money,' Kaali Pandey comforted her.

Sweety's phone began to ring. It was Lallan.

'The time has come! Ghonchu will take you for your driving lessons. You will feel thirsty at Gol Ghar. You will ask Ghonchu to get water,' Kaali said.

'I know, I know. We have rehearsed it so many times now, Papa. The moment Ghonchu is away, a van will come and bump into my car. I'll get angry and get out of the car to shout at them, and then I will be pulled into the van—officially kidnapped!'

'Don't get too excited. This could very well backfire on us! The police should not find out!' Kaali Pandey warned her.

'Don't worry, Papa. Let me show you that your daughter has a mind of her own.' Sweety patted her father's shoulder.

'I am risking my daughter—' Kaali's eyes began to water.

'It's nothing. I will be back in a week. I want to see my father win!' Sweety held his hands and squeezed them lightly. 'Ghonchu is waiting outside. Lallan has the road map,' Kaali said.

Sweety opened the suitcase, pulled out a chiffon sari and kept it in the bag. 'Why are you taking that?' asked Kaali. 'It gives me a lot of strength,' Sweety smiled.

'Get rid of this burkha. You will make people suspicious,' Kaali added. Sweety sighed and took it off. They hugged each other.

The mighty Kaali Pandey's heart melted. His chest was heaving. He could not bear to see his Sweety going away. No kidnapping had started on such a good note in all of human history!

33

The kidnapping had gone off without a hitch. Sweety was with Lallan. She had been gagged in a car and was a bit dazed by the chloroform.

As she opened her eyes, she saw Lallan's petrified face in a blur. He was driving.

'You are sweating, my dear kidnapper,' Sweety teased him. 'Don't joke, Sweety! You have made a joke of my life!' Lallan wasn't wearing the Ray Ban now, yet he had the courage to look Sweety in the eye when he spoke to her.

'It's cool. See, I got your business running! Tomorrow, the news will flash that I have been kidnapped and just imagine my ransom—five crores! My poor father will cry his lungs out and thank god that he insured me. He will get his five crores from the business model and you will walk away with many high-profile clients!' Sweety's pink lips still looked like roses to Lallan. They always distracted him.

'We are few miles away from Motihari. We go there and cross the Nepal border. Our hideout is ready. Just be careful,' Lallan told her sternly, focusing on driving in the low light. 'Take a U-turn. We need to go somewhere else,' Sweety said.

'I am not listening to you. Everything will go as per the plan,' Lallan was curt and sharp. 'Step on the brake,' Sweety tried to grab his hand. 'Stay away while I am driving.' Lallan pushed her back a little with his elbow.

Sweety pulled him by his collar and kissed him. Lallan lost control, and the car came to halt with a screech of the brakes. That wet kiss and the sandalwood smell overshadowed the odour of sweat and the chloroform in the car.

'Chill, today we are not in danger. My kidnapping has not been announced yet.'

'Sweety, you will destroy both of us.' Lallan had her face in his hands. Sweety looked at him with love in her eyes. 'Don't look at me like this. I am committing a crime. You are making me commit a crime. You are taking undue advantage of my weakness,' Lallan said helplessly.

'See, we both have a shining future. Don't panic. Just listen to me carefully. We are not going to the place we were supposed to go.' Sweety was very clear in her mind about the change of plan.

'Your father will go mad!' Lallan had his reservations about this.

'No, trust my intuition. I think we will be caught there. I want to hide somewhere else. A place that only both of us are aware of,' said Sweety.

'Where?' Lallan stared at her.

A stalled truck was visible ahead. Sweety was eyeing it. 'It's going to MP,' Sweety read the number plate. 'You want to go to Madhya Pradesh?' Lallan asked.

'Mumbai.'

'Oh, Mumbai, of course!' Lallan said sarcastically. Sweety smiled and nodded. 'And then, my Madhuri Dixit, you will participate in *Jhalak Dikhla Ja*,' Lallan joked.

'You are not taking me seriously,' Sweety sulked.

'You are a stubborn girl. Life doesn't function like this,' Lallan tried to put his hand on her shoulder.

They could see people loading sacks into the truck ahead. 'Have you seen *Highway*?' Sweety asked. 'I don't see Hindi films these days,' Lallan tried to change the topic.

'You must have seen *Dil*. Or *Qayamat Se Qayamat Tak*?' Sweety asked him with a sparkle in her eyes. 'Yes. So what?' Lallan did not want to participate in any of her stupid games.

'Going by truck is the best way to reach Mumbai. We hop on any truck. How romantic it would be! It wouldn't even feel like a kidnapping!'

'You want to get me killed?'

Sweety leaned towards him, once again. Lallan applied the brakes. It reminded them of the early-morning driving classes filled with romance and danger.

'Don't do this to me,' Lallan pleaded.

Sweety didn't give a damn. She bit his ear. Lallan felt morphined. Their lips met once again.

Sweety took out a chloroformed handkerchief from her purse.

'I can put chloroform on your face and kidnap you!' Sweety warned him.

'You are threatening me.' Lallan's anxiety reached new heights.

'Whatever! Follow me! You have no other option.'

Lallan held her and ran his fingers through the cascade of her tangled hair.

They kissed in the dim light.

34

They were tucked inside the truck, among the sacks filled with tomatoes. Sweety was excited; Lallan was frightened. 'I'm covered in tomato puree,' Sweety whispered, wiping off tomato pulp from her arms. 'What if we get caught?' Lallan whispered back hoarsely. He sat stiffly, packed between the tomato sacks which smelt like a room full of raw ketchup.

The truck sped along the highway, rocking like a landing plane at times.

'Why are we going to Mumbai? Where will we stay?' Lallan looked worried.

Sweety was playful. She looked like a kid who had just got out of boarding school. 'I am hungry.' She made a face and picked out a tomato. She searched for her purse and took out few sachets of Domino's oregano and red chilli flakes.

'I can make anything exotic!' Sweety exclaimed. She tried opening the packets but could not as her hands were slippery with tomato pulp. Lallan tore off the corner of the sachets with his teeth and sprinkled the oregano and chilli flakes on Sweety's tomato.

'Now eat!' Lallan looked away.

'I like Italian food.' Sweety happily bit into the herbed tomato.

Lallan did not respond.

'I always collect extra sachets from the pizza guy. I use them all.' Sweety smiled. 'Don't sulk, my handsome hulk.'

Lallan held her by her chin.

'You are taking some kind of revenge, aren't you?' Lallan looked frustrated.

'We will go to Mumbai. We both will have an escape. A good time! Let's enjoy for a week,' Sweety tried to convince him.

Lallan wasn't buying it.

'Will we sleep on the streets in Mumbai? Do you want the plan to fail?' Lallan asked Sweety.

'I have a friend in Mumbai. He is getting me a flat for the hideout.' Sweety had things ready.

'You have told about this plan to some outsider? Are you out of your mind?' Lallan felt like shouting at her but only grumbled.

Sweety rested her head on his shoulder. Lallan shivered in the cold. She pulled a chiffon sari out of her bag and wrapped it around both of them.

'Sari?' Lallan looked at her inquisitively.

'That's the only thing I am carrying.' Sweety smiled.

'For? ' Lallan looked at her.

'It's my mother's sari. I sleep with it every day.' Sweety smiled through the tears.

'Your mother committed suicide.'

'How long can a bird live in a cage?'

'You want to leave the cage?' Lallan looked at Sweety.

Sweety nodded and there was a simple smile on her face. Her face and eyes looked divine even with her devilish plan.

'The chloroform was too strong. I am still sleepy,' Sweety yawned.

She rested her light head on his broad shoulder. Lallan's frozen shoulders eased up for the moment.

The tomato sacks were pushing the lovers towards each other, gently.

35

Meetu's parents were at Lallan's home. The hot tea had turned into a cold drink. Plates of chooda mattar with crisp-fried onions were as decorated as it could be. Food diplomacy had taken a back seat and it was the time for rishta diplomacy.

'Your son has the audacity to say no to my daughter!' Meetu's father was furious.

'You know how he is. Momentary fluctuations of a young boy,' Lallan's father tried to pacify his would-be kin.

'Give me the money I had once given you to rescue your kidnapped son,' Meetu's father demanded as his birthright.

'How can we? You know about our business!' Lallan's father tried to explain his financial limitations.

'Now your son is a millionaire. He has high-profile clients. Now why can't you pay us?'

'It's too soon. It's just been few days. We don't even know how things will shape up for now,' Lallan's father politely justified.

Lallan's mother wanted to cut the cold vibe short. She extended the plate of chooda mattar to Meetu's father and mother.

'Meetu has not eaten since yesterday,' Meetu's mother refused to take the plate of snacks.

'We thought that we are investing on our son—in-law but he doesn't seem to be interested all of a sudden. This is breach of trust!' Meetu's father got up in anger. Her mother followed suit.

'He has made our daughter cry. Now we don't mind if your smiles fade away. We need our money back in fifteen days,' Meetu's father announced.

36

It was six in the morning when the truck stopped at a dhaba in Itarsi. Sweety peeped out. She shook Lallan awake. 'Get up! We need to hop out!'

'Where are we?' Lallan was in a daze.

'Near a dhaba.' Sweety sounded happy.

'Where from here?' Lallan was looking like a surrendered driver.

'We will have to take another truck to Mumbai, just get off this one,' Sweety ordered in a whisper.

Lallan's phone rang. It was Ghonchu.

'Now? Ghonchu is calling. They must have cross-checked with the people in Nepal. They must be in panic now.' Lallan sounded very scared.

'Let it ring, don't pick up now. This is a kidnapping case. It isn't that easy, is it?'

Ghonchu's call stopped suddenly.

'Battery drained.' Lallan looked helpless.

'Jump out now!' ordered Sweety.

She crumpled the sari and put it back in the bag. They were ready to jump off the truck. It was still quite dark and cold. They jumped out with a sack of tomato falling after them. Tomatoes scattered all over. One or two tomatoes got smashed by their feet as they tried to move quickly out of the sight.

37

Kaali Pandey was at his residence with his party members. Tension mounted in the house.

'It's been fifteen hours!' Kaali Pandey looked anxious like a whale gasping in a pond.

'New inspector has been instructed. We only need to wait for the ransom call.' A middle-aged party member, Sudhanshu Yadav, tried to activate the best device to maintain the peace and sanity.

Ghonchu stood still beside Kaali like a rock.

'Ghonchu . . . You really have no clue?' asked another young member of the party, Guddu Singh.

Ghonchu looked scared.

'I don't believe it. He was with Sweety didi,' the member emphasized again.

Kaali Pandey did not like his trusted henchman to be suspected.

'Perhaps she planned to elope or . . .' grumbled Guddu Singh, who was nowhere close to being loyal to Kaali Pandey.

'Get up and buzz off right away!' Kaali roared.

All the party members felt the tremors aloud.

'Right now!' Kaali shooed the young man away.

Ghonchu got a glass of water for Kaali.

'I want my daughter back, no matter what.' Kaali looked restless.

'We can just wait for the ransom call. The best part is that you got her insured for kidnapping.' Sudhanshu Yadav tried to reassure the untamed Kaali Pandey.

'I never thought that ten days after her insurance, my daughter would be kidnapped.' Kaali looked helpless.

'It must have backfired.' Sudhanshu Yadav could sense some loopholes.

'I will find my daughter. No one can mess with Minister Kaali Pandey!'

'I suspect Radhey Shyam Yadav,' Sudhanshu Yadav warned Kaali.

'He will not see the light of the next day, if he has done so.'

There was a silence for a few minutes, when the landline rang.

38

This new truck was filthy. It was carrying ice and fishes.

'Why have we taken this one?' asked Sweety holding her nose.

'This one is going to Mumbai. Simple,' said Lallan.

'Stinking fish,' Sweety complained holding her breath.

'You can't be picky,' Lallan mocked her.

'We choose our own destiny,' Sweety tried to be philosophical.

'Destiny dictates us, at least for me!' Lallan gasped.

Drums shook as fishes quivered inside.

'You see the fish in the drum . . . quivering?' asked Sweety.

'There is less oxygen for them,' said Lallan calmly.

'You were also a fish in a drum with less oxygen, struggling and quivering. I want to give you the sea.' Sweety held his cold palms.

'What if someone doesn't want the sea?' Lallan asked Sweety.

'Everyone wants the sea. Some are just afraid of it,' Sweety muttered, looking at Lallan's lost expression. 'Tides, the depth, sharks, the salt . . . what scares you?' Sweety started playing with his palm. Lallan felt a current run through his palm to his head. He withdrew his hands.

'You know what, Lallan? You are naive. You have eyes, you have a mind, you have a heart, and you have a dream . . . but you don't have one thing which is most important,' Sweety was slowly getting him into conversation. 'You don't have self-belief!' Her curly hair framed her face; her eyes were smoky.

They were close.

'I want to gift you that belief.'

'Who am I to you?' Lallan was not sure if he was being hypnotized or intimidated.

'You are my kidnapper.' Sweety came as close to him as she could.

'I have been forced to,' said Lallan controlling his breath.

'No, you actually believe in me. You believe in the universe's conspiracy. Like Shah Rukh Khan, you believe in destiny. You believe in love, but you don't believe in yourself!' Sweety interlocked her palm in his.

'I want you to cry and wash out the tsunami which has built up inside you for ages. That tsunami is against my father, against the system, against your helplessness, against the curse of your destiny.'

Nobody had ever spoken to Lallan like this.

'You have never cried all your life. You have acted strong. Cry today. Become weak for a moment and you will be strong for ever!' Sweety touched his elbow and covered it with her soft hand.

Lallan's eyes became moist. Tears started rolling down his cheeks.

'Don't stop,' Sweety spoke softly.

Flood of tears ushered down like monsoon had just poured in the winter. Amongst the quivering fish drums, two souls quivered and shivered too. They hugged each other tightly. They were one for a moment. A moment that looked eternal. Lallan and Sweety had a storm of emotions whirling around them like a coursing wind.

Lovers are like the wind; one can predict them perhaps but never control.

39

It was not the ransom call. There was a man crying at the other end of the line.

It was Ghonchu's friend Natku who was screaming like a loudspeaker at an election rally.

'I ate isabgol but my stomach is still on fire. I think I will die tonight!' he screamed on the phone. He had an indigestion problem and needed Ghonchu to attend to him urgently.

'It's urgent here. Take a rickshaw, hold your stomach and go to the Sadar Hospital,' Ghonchu whispered.

Minister Kaali Pandey sat disappointed, knowing that this was also not the call he awaited. Meanwhile, Ghonchu was still struggling to find excuses.

'Ghonchu . . . Go!' Kaali Pandey ordered him as if some major general was ordering his soldier to go to the warfront.

Ghonchu was not sure if it was a taunt or a serious order from his monster master. He kept the receiver right on the place.

'We haven't got the call yet.' Kaali Pandey looked nervous.

'The policemen are working on it. You know how it is, don't you?' Sudhanshu Yadav thought that this was the best time to ally with his leader.

Sudhanshu Yadav was preparing himself to be the frontrunner in the second line of leadership in Minister Kaali Pandey's den. He never wanted to cross Kaali Pandey's line of authority but he always was Kaali's immediate disciple.

'You may go too. Leave me alone. I will handle it,' Kaali ordered in his grave voice.

'I am your younger brother, na? Sweety is like a daughter to me too. I can't sleep and snore peacefully until I find her.' Sudhanshu tried to score a brownie point.

'It's my fate; let me deal with it. You keep a strong eye on Radhey Shyam,' Kaali Pandey instructed.

Sudhanshu Yadav got up and touched Kaali Pandey's feet and left. Ghonchu was all alone with Kaali Pandey.

'I called up Lallan. His mobile phone is off,' Ghonchu complained.

Kaali looked all around.

'I think it's a double-cross,' Kaali muttered.

'No, sir, I don't know anything,' Ghonchu pleaded.

He knew that fingers were being pointed at him. His friend Natku's call had made it worse.

'I trust you more than my heart,' Kaali Pandey tried to pacify Ghonchu.

'I swear I don't know about Sweety didi . . . where did she go and . . .' Ghonchu was trying to give a wide range of possible justifications.

'It's Lallan. I think he is double-crossing us,' Kaali said with authority.

'Meaning?' Ghonchu looked confused. He never gave his assumptions first. That was his trait. He too thought it was Lallan but he didn't want to say it in the beginning. After all, Ghonchu had grown up in the political company of big monsters like Kaali Pandey and his goons of all shapes and sizes.

'I have not revealed a very big secret to you, a very big truth. This kidnapping is a proxy one,' Kaali told the truth to Ghonchu.

'We needed money. You know Sweety was insured. I involved Lallan,' Minister Kaali Pandey explained.

Ghonchu's mouth was wide open.

'So they should have reached Nepal long back where I arranged a hideout for them. They have not. Lallan's phone is also switched off and . . .' Kaali Pandey looked defeated even before the war was declared.

'Now?' Ghonchu could not understand the scripted kidnapping game and its possible consequences.

'Now, I am jacked. I have not got the ransom call yet. We will wait for twelve more hours, and if he doesn't call, we are in a soup!' Minister Kaali Pandey looked puzzled by his own deed.

'Don't worry, Sarkar; Lallan doesn't have the *aukaat* of going to that extent.' Ghonchu opened his small mouth wide for the first time.

'But where have they gone? We will have to find out soon! Or is it someone else double-crossing us?' Kaali's mind wandered.

Ghonchu squatted on the floor, his mind calculating the math of this new-found kidnapping news.

'We can only wait for few more hours,' said the much worried Kaali Pandey.

Minister Kaali Pandey was never found this helpless. He felt like the captain of a football team whose player has scored against his own team. His biggest source of helplessness was the compulsive confidentiality he had to maintain to save his face in society. Along with many other things, it was also a major tussle of ego for him now.

Kaali Pandey also had the fear of losing his powerful image if this news reached the media. This could jeopardize his chances of winning the upcoming elections. After all, how could you vote for someone to safeguard his constituency if he is not able to protect his own daughter?

Minister Kaali Pandey for once appeared to be the king of a castle made out of sand.

40

It was fairly dark inside the truck. Beams of sunlight fell on their faces.

'You look as beautiful in the sunlight as in the moonlight,' Lallan said, tucking her locks behind her ears.

Sweety was leaning on the drum with fish splashing inside. Lallan leaned over Sweety. The resistance in him had flushed out. He was like a fish, not of the drum but of the sea! Lallan was fearless for the first time. He wanted to flow like the wind at the moment.

He looked deep into Sweety's eyes.

'Do you actually love me?' Lallan asked her.

'What do you think?' Sweety asked him.

'I have never trusted anyone,' Lallan answered.

'Do you trust me?' Sweety asked.

'I was enslaved by your father. I never thought I would ever be able to look his daughter in the eye.' Lallan cleared the slight lump in his throat.

'Revenge taken!' Sweety smiled.

'No. I am loyal. We will reach Mumbai and I am going to call him,' Lallan said firmly.

'I like your loyalty,' Sweety said buttoning his collar.

'Ow, that hurts!' Lallan moved away.

Sweety dragged him by his neck.

'Learn! You will soon have to knot a tie, Mr Would-be Ambani!' Sweety teased.

They were engrossed with each other when the truck stopped with a jerk. Sweety and Lallan got scared. They ducked inside. They could hear faint voices outside.

'There is one drum. It has your arms.' The voice of the man talking was squeaky.

'Ustaad, only you can do this, machhli ka kaanta,' said one another.

'Macchli ka kaanta or machhli ka katta?' the driver joked, referring to country-made pistol, the katta.

Both voices drew closer. Lallan and Sweety tried to squeeze in as much as possible. Their hearts were pounding fast. The footsteps were getting closer. The voices were louder and clearer now. Lallan and Sweety held each other's hand as if they were to jump off a cliff. Nut and bolts of the truck's back loosened up and the shutter rolled up in a sudden flash. The sunlight streamed in like floodlight, blinding the lovers squeezed inside. They knew that there was no escape now.

The two truck drivers pulled themselves up into the back of the truck.

'Rohu?' asked another voice which sounded like a jarring tractor.

'No. Mangur!' corrected the truck driver in his squeaky voice.

They both made their way to the last drum where Lallan and Sweety were hiding. As they tried to peep in, they saw feet with sports shoes and open laces.

'Who is that? Someone there?' asked the truck driver raising his voice. He tried to grab Lallan by his collar. 'What honeymoon is happening here? Who are you guys?' he screamed.

The truck driver was reeking of cheap alcohol in the middle of the day.

'Hold the girl!' ordered the other guy.

'Chain this guy,' said the driver who had tried to grab Lallan.

Lallan pushed away the fish drum and the driver got hit by it. Fish fell out of the drum. The truck became wet and slippery.

The men tried to get hold of Sweety. Her shoelaces got tangled as she tried to walk away. The truck driver got back to his feet. The other man had Lallan by his collar.

'Who are you? What you are doing here?' The other man banged his head on a fish drum.

'Drag them out!' the truck driver shouted at the other man.

Lallan tried to hold the wooden rail of the tailgate of the truck but his hands were slippery.

'Lallan, run!' shouted Sweety as she saw the other man going to stump his head with a brick that had been lying there to stabilize the drum.

Lallan jabbed the man with his elbows. The brick fell on top of another drum. The truck driver had Sweety by her arms. Sweety took a fish and slid it into the truck driver's shirt. The man jumped around.

'Lallan, aren't you a hero?' Sweety shouted at Lallan.

Lallan was almost entangled in the arms of the other guy. He was struggling hard to squeeze out but could not.

Sweety had almost freed herself and, before the man could attack again, she pulled the chloroformed handkerchief out of Lallan's pocket and pressed it against the face of the guy holding him. The man became dizzy at once. He freed Lallan's hand and, before he could help himself, he fell down.

The truck driver turned furious. He took out the big desi katta from the fish drum and pointed straight at Lallan Jha.

'I will shoot you right now!' he yelled.

'And what will you get out of that?' Lallan asked.

'Nothing.' It was brutally simple.

'Then instead of killing us, you could get something from us,' Sweety proposed.

'Like what?' the man looked at her inquisitively.

She removed her wristwatch. 'This is from the US. Christian Dior. Not less than five lakhs in India,' announced Sweety and handed the watch over to the driver.

Lallan was astonished to see Sweety dealing with criminals with such ease.

Being able to negotiate with outlaws was quite a natural personality trait in Sweety. She was fearless. Besides, it ran in her blood.

'Lallan, take off your shoes. I think it will fit you, Sardarji. Your feet are swollen. Please don't wear these Hawaii chappals,' Sweety ordered Lallan to follow immediately.

Lallan took off his shoes and exchanged them for the Hawaii chappals of the truck driver. This barter system was nothing new for a middle-class small towner like Lallan. His mother used to cook and pack delicacies for her neighbours and they would always return her utensils with food in it.

'See, we are running away from our homes. Just for our shaadi . . .' Sweety tried to explain. She took off her gold earrings and offered those as well. 'You may take these too,' she said handing them over. 'Twenty-two-carat gold, American diamonds. I don't think they are real,' Sweety added.

The truck driver was overwhelmed by their honesty.

'You must be thirsty. Do you want some water?' asked the driver. He felt he had to offer something in lieu of the many things he was receiving.

Lallan and Sweety got out of the truck. The truck driver climbed up to his seat and got a bottle of water. Sweety gulped it down fearlessly. Lallan was still hesitant.

'It's okay, ji. But you shouldn't have done that to my friend,' the truck driver complained.

'It's a light one . . . He will be okay,' Lallan interfered.

'Marriage sharriage?' enquired the truck driver.

They both nodded.

'I will drop you in Mumbai. Just don't talk about the guns to anyone,' said the guy.

'And you don't talk about us with anyone,' Lallan added his part.

'Done deal,' said the driver and got ready to drive.

'Sit in the front. Mumbai is 200 km,' Sardarji insisted.

'We feel like we're sitting on the seashore when we sit at the back with fish all around. We'd prefer that.' Sweety sounded adorable.

'Okay, take care of my friend. When will he wake up?'

'In an hour. It's very little chloroform. You can use it for your wife, when she picks up a fight,' Sweety joked.

Sardarji didn't know whether to laugh or to take offence.

'Let's go or we will be late,' Lallan wanted to cut Sweety short and generally avoid small talk.

'Do you have something to eat?' asked Sweety. Lallan did not really like Sweety getting too friendly with this guy.

'Actually, the last truck had tomatoes, I could eat. But you just have fish,' Sweety complained as if she was denied her birthright.

'I have mixture, ji.' Sardarji couldn't say no to such a hungry and beautiful girl.

Regular truck drivers on the highway are a self-sufficient lot. They carry their share of alcohol and all kinds of snacks with them. They often stop at highway dhabas to have food, but are always loaded with drinks.

'Ya, ya; I don't mind that.' Sweety extended her hand.

'I have some *tharra*, local drinks, too,' Sardarji got overfriendly.

'That will quench some burning thirst, yes!' said Sweety.

Lallan looked at her with bulging eyes. He was quite uncomfortable at that given point of time. He had initially enjoyed Sweety's initiatives in order to save the situation but it was gradually getting on his nerves.

Sweety got the hint. 'Oh, it's Tuesday! I will not be able to drink. I'm so sorry,' she said.

'Ok, ji. Hop on.' Sardarji directed them towards the back of the truck.

Sweety and Lallan finally found a small, dry patch within the fishy wetlands of the truck.

41

Kaali was not in his Ambassador. He was in an old Contessa model. His car stopped at Lallan's home. Ghonchu followed him. Lallan's father opened the door when he heard the sound of the car. It was late evening by now. He was surprised to see Kaali Pandey here. Kaali looked more hurried than usual, more nervous than usual, more aggressive than his usual self.

'Saheb, anything urgent that you had to come in person?' Sati Nath Jha asked, opening the door for him.

'Lallan is acting oversmart.' Kaali Pandey looked sternly in his eyes.

'What do you mean?' Jha looked confused.

'I blessed him with the freedom to live and he has gone and destroyed it all! This is going to turn out to be really bad,' Kaali warned them.

'Please tell me what has happened,' Jha looked apologetic before even knowing his son's offence.

'He told you that he is going to Delhi, right?'

'Yes, yes . . . he did . . . You know his work. You have trust in him— '

'And you know that my daughter has been kidnapped, and also that I had insured her?' Kaali grunted.

'Yes. But then, why are you angry with Lallan? He is doing his job, right?' Jha said hesitantly. He had some belief in his son for the time being.

'Have you spoken to him since he left?' asked Kaali.

'No.' Jha ji looked little frightened.

'He is playing tricks with me! If he acts oversmart, he will be killed!'

'But what has happened? You should tell me.' Jha was petrified.

'You will get to know soon, what your son has gotten himself into—very soon! It's going to be worse now. I kidnapped him long ago. Now I will get him murdered!' Kaali's voice shook the house.

He stormed out, back to his Contessa, and drove off.

Meetu was up and was sitting at her window. She saw Kaali Pandey leaving Lallan's house. She could sense something— something which had left the Jha's house in a pall of doom.

42

Mumbai.

It was late September, not very cold. It was the time when clouds had rained enough and winter was still shy about coming in.

A humid and hurried Mumbai was working to its own rhythm. Loudspeakers all over were blaring Ganpati bhajans.

Lallan and Sweety were deposited at the Crawford market, famed for its gothic architecture. It's also one of the biggest wholesale markets for fresh fruits, vegetables, poultry and grocery in south Mumbai.

Sweety did all that a kidnapped girl would never do. In her script, she was the free soul who could change the course of things at any time. She was the director of her own movie.

She took a selfie with the Sardarji. She hugged him and took out some five hundred–rupee notes from the pachranga achaar bag that her father had given her and handed him over as gift.

'Thank you, ji; thank you. See? We became friends.' Sardarji smiled.

'Why don't you give him your gold chain, Lallan? He has helped us so much,' Sweety asked Lallan. Lallan didn't like the way Sweety was behaving. He took his thin gold chain off and handed it over to Sardarji.

'God will give you both a lot of wealth!' the greedy truck driver thanked them and moved on.

Lallan and Sweety then walked out of the Crawford market. It was the second day of the Ganpati festival and the city was filled with Ganpati idols in all sizes and poses. Lallan and Sweety got into a black-and-yellow taxi and looked out of the windows. Sweety's hair was tangled and flew in all directions.

The taxi driver was silent till they all reached the Haji Ali Dargah. But then, realizing that they were in Mumbai for the first time, he switched to tour guide mode.

'Haji Ali Dargah is one of the most popular religious places in Mumbai, visited by people of all religions and faith alike,' he announced. 'See, that is the Sea Link.'

Lallan stared the Worli Sea Link in the distance.

'And that's Antilla, the world-famous Ambani house!'

Lallan stuck out his neck to see the much talked about Antilla, owned by the inspiration of his life, Mukesh Ambani. 'Most expensive house in the world!' boasted the taxi driver.

Lallan and Sweety stared at the house. 'Slums all around. Yuck, my house is better off,' Sweety mocked. 'Where are you from? UP, Bihar?' the driver asked. 'Madhya Pradesh, Jabalpur.' Sweety sounded extra curt, contrary to her style.

'That's the beauty of Mumbai—among the slums, there rises a tall building.'

Lallan and Sweety smiled at each other. It was an achievement that they had finally reached Mumbai after all the hurdles along the way. It had been well over twenty-four hours now. Almost thirty-six, in fact. They knew that Kaali Pandey must be going crazy by now.

They had now been together for one day and one night, living every moment of it all together, with each other. This soul-stirring kidnapping journey had brought them closer together.

'You see, the denser the slum, the taller the building, the more expensive it gets. I came to Mumbai from Samastipur in Bihar to become a hero in the Hindi film industry. And see what I have become,' the taxi driver went on.

'So you never tried?' asked Sweety. 'I tried madam, I was in *Shahenshah*,' boasted the guy. 'With Amitabh Bachchan?' Sweety was pleasantly surprised.

'Yes, but I was standing in a crowd of some two hundred people,' the cab driver clarified. 'That's it?' Lallan asked. 'Ya, that's it. You have to drive your body, you need to get the fuel, you need to earn money—everything has a cost,' the driver was getting philosophical.

They were driving on the Worli Sea Link now. 'See! It's the Sea Link! You might have seen this in the films,' the driver said.

'So you got the fish to the sea?' Lallan joked.

'Now I can jump into the sea. I hope you will not get lost.' Sweety looked at him. Her half smile looked dangerous.

'This link has become a suicide point nowadays,' the taxi driver chipped in. They chose to ignore him. 'People stop their cars and just jump,' the driver added.

'How far is Yari Road?' Sweety enquired. 'It will take some forty minutes from here,' taxi driver replied, stepping on the accelerator.

Sweety and Lallan devoured the city with their eyes. 'Near Mandir–Masjid Marg on Yari Road?' the driver asked. 'Yes, around that,' Lallan said. 'Pegasus Apartments,' Sweety whispered to him. Lallan did not want give out the details of where they were going to anyone. Sweety, on the other hand, kept forgetting that she was supposed to have been kidnapped.

'Can we stop somewhere? I need to get a guitar,' Sweety said. Lallan glared at her. 'No, I mean, I wanted to get it, but I could not and now I really want it,' she insisted.

'Wow, madam. It doesn't look like you play the guitar!' the driver said.

'Even you don't look like a hero!' Sweety retorted. 'I just meant that pop stars look different. You are from MP,' he tried to control the damage.

'I can give Britney Spears a run for her money! But I know you would not know who she is!' Sweety said, getting angry. Lallan held her hand and tried to calm her down.

'Madam, you can show off in MP. Not here.' He stopped the taxi just as the Worli Sea Link ended.

'Get down, Lallan. A bloody taxiwala speaking to Sweety like this. Sweety Pandey!' she shouted.

Lallan was getting worried—the taxi driver now knew her name. He got out of the taxi, pulled Sweety out, and handed the taxi driver a couple of hundred-rupee notes. 'Keep the change.'

The taxi driver had a very big ego, as big as Amitabh Bachchan in *Shahenshah*. His eyes were as intense as Amitabh Bachchan in *Deewar* but he chose not to speak a single word. Anyone could predict that if at all he was to say anything he would have said the famous dialogue of Amitabh Bachchan from *Deewar*, 'Mai aaj bhi pheke huwe paise nahi uthata.' He slapped away the money, started his taxi and moved away.

Lallan and Sweety stood stranded on the road, aghast at what had just happened to them!

'The guitar can wait,' Lallan told her.

There is an interesting trait in the girls from the powerful families of the badlands in Bihar. They sometimes love being dominated by their men. Sweety also loved when Lallan was strict with her, for reasons that only she knew . . .

43

Radhe Radhe, Serpentine Road, Patna

This was the address of Radhey Shyam Yadav's office inside his residential campus. The campus had a little temple dedicated to Lord Krishna. All visitors had to first come to this temple and take the god's blessings before meeting Yadav. This was the custom that had been followed in the Yadav mansion for decades. Krishna is considered to be the *isht dev*, or family deity, of the Yadavs in Uttar Pradesh and Bihar.

Radhey Shyam Yadav's system was so famous in the area that it had become a legend. It was said that once, in the 1980s, police had raided Yadav's home and all his men requested the police team to come via the temple. The police had to listen to them but then their boss had to spend some extra time in prison.

There was a strange trend in that part of the land that everyone in the underworld—dons, criminals-turned-politicians or anybody with an illegal background—were usually very religious. Maybe they wanted to keep a clear and transparent account of their sins and virtues.

Radhey Shyam Yadav was busy playing teen patti, a popular card game, with a guest, surrounded by henchmen on guard. A dozen half-naked, dhoti-clad priests were performing the aarti in his temple, chanting mantras in a very high pitch. Radhey Shyam glowered at the priests and they fell silent.

Radhey Shyam Yadav was very happy to show this off to Sudhanshu Yadav—his special guest for the day.

'So, you will always play second fiddle to Pandeyji?' ridiculed Radhey Shyam Yadav, shuffling the cards in his hand.

'Are you sure you won't mind losing?' Sudhanshu Yadav retorted, throwing a card on the table.

'Yadavs never lose, Sudhanshu Babu. Even my defeat will be the victory of a Yadav, Sudhanshu Yadav!' Radhey Shyam Yadav replied, putting down his card of choice.

'Are you afraid of his higher caste? You are second to none. Yadavs are the new rulers. Look at how I feed these so called Babajis. They will promptly stand up if I give them a sharp look,' Radhey Shyam Yadav gloated.

Caste has always been used as a device to politicize issues and polarize votes for power in India. Bihar is no exception. Radhey Shyam Yadav had always wanted this meeting with Minister Kaali Pandey's second-in-command.

Manohar Lal Pal, Radhey Shyam's manager for the past three decades, was puzzled, thinking, 'How come I didn't know Sudhanshu Yadav would be here?'

Sudhanshu Yadav was sharp enough to read the atmosphere around him. He noticed that Pal looked stressed and confused. 'Pal Babu, don't take tension about your saheb losing in the game of cards. I have bigger and better games for him to win in life!' Sudhanshu Yadav teased.

'And that is?' Radhey Shyam Yadav did not want to let any opportunity go waste.

'Are Radhey Shyam Babu, why don't you disclose minister saheb's tape that you have? That can not only get him defeated in the upcoming elections but also land him straight in jail,' Sudhanshu suggested.

Radhey Shyam seemed to be engrossed in his own thoughts for a while. Suddenly his mobile phone rang. 'Minister Kaali Pandey calling' flashed on the screen. Radhey Shyam shook his head and picked up the phone.

'Arrey Pandeyji, you really have a very long life. I was just thinking about you,' Radhey Shyam said. The voice from the other side was not of Kaali Pandey. It was Ghonchu.

'Maalik is very unwell. He is lying down. He wanted me to use his phone to inform you, saheb, that it will take some more time.'

'But there has to be a deadline! When will he fulfil his promise?' Radhey Shyam asked impatiently. 'That is something only Maalik can say. I will inform him, saheb.' Ghonchu knew his role well.

Radhey Shyam was irritated. He tried to re-arrange his thoughts, but this time, the expression on his face had changed. Radhey Shyam Yadav was not an easy nut to crack. He did not believe what he had been told. His mind started working faster. 'Find out from the police if they have got any clue about minister saheb's daughter's kidnapping. I need to take this case up personally. It's high time now!' he announced.

Radhey Shyam knew Kaali Pandey in and out. They had grown up together, partnering in the same crimes. They had come up with many conspiracies together. They had been a deadly combination. In fact, they had become a very reliable crime syndicate as far as the kidnapping industry was concerned. The media had started referring to the 'kidnapping industry' in the badlands only after this gang took it to the next level in terms of the revenue they generated.

Something had just crossed Radhey Shyam Yadav's mind. Something very serious that could have very serious and deadly consequences.

'Why are you bothered about money? I'll pay double the amount for revealing what you want to hide,' Sudhanshu Yadav said. Radhey Shyam was tempted by the offer.

Yadavs united in the name of caste. Kaali's loss was Radhey Shyam Yadav's gain. Teen patti was soon to be replaced by a game of snakes and ladders in which no one was beyond evil.

44

Pegasus Apartments was a high-rise with deck-sized apartments near Mandir-Masjid Marg at Yari Road in Versova, Mumbai. This is a unique road very close to the Versova beach, where Muslims and Hindus live in peace. Mandir-Masjid Marg is also known for being an area where flats are conveniently rented out to unmarried couples who want to live together, irrespective of their caste, community, culture or creed. The area is quite close to the Madh Island—a beautiful hang-out for couples and families. Versova Beach and Madh Island take us back to the Bollywood films of the seventies and a little bit of the eighties, when Ajit used to play the character of a smuggler and all his gold used to arrive at either Versova Beach or Madh Island.

The tall Pegasus Apartments building was like a pencil standing amid small old buildings that were dying a slow death. The reception area oozed opulence. Most of names on the board were of Sheikhs. Sweety and Lallan went inside, keeping up a pretence of indifference. Sweety had a guitar in her hand. A brand new guitar.

'I think it's a Muslim society.' Lallan looked a bit apprehensive.

'You are so typical. It's Mumbai. Don't think like a Patna boy now!' Sweety chided him.

She strode straight in and entered the lift. She confidently pressed the button for the fourteenth floor.

'How come the guard didn't stop you?' Lallan asked.

'Confidence.' Sweety winked at him.

They reached the fourteenth floor. She walked to flat number 1402 as confidently as if it had belonged to her father. She counted the potted plants kept outside. 'One, two, three four,' she stopped at the fourth one. She lifted the pot with the tiny cactus. There was a small key tucked under it.

Sweety took out the key, opened the door of the flat and led Lallan into it. She looked around, went to a little cupboard and opened it. There were a bunch of switches hidden within it. She flipped the third one. Suddenly, the lights and fans came on.

Lallan looked at her, amazed. 'Have you come here before?' he asked. 'No. My friend told me everything. It's his friend's flat,' Sweety replied, pouring out a glass of water from a jug on the dining table.

Sweety decided to explore the flat. She peeped into the kitchen and started laughing. Lallan wondered what it was! Sweety pointed at the finger bowl-sized basin and laughed some more.

'You are a mad girl. It is so difficult to predict what makes you angry and what makes you laugh!' Lallan said, amused.

'Mumbai is like a match box, na?' Sweety smiled as she opened the tiny tap. 'It looks like a finger bowl. This is the smallest wash basin, I have ever seen!' She went from the pygmy kitchen to the bathroom. She ran the shower and promptly got drenched.

Lallan blushed. 'I am not being shy, but someone else is!' Sweety teased him.

'Come!' She pulled Lallan inside.

They both got drenched. Lallan's head hit the shower a bit.

'Duck, duck, it's a pint-sized bathroom!' Sweety was ecstatic!

Lallan looked at her face. He smiled.

'You look so happy when you smile!' Sweety pinched his cheeks.

'Everyone looks happy when they smile,' Lallan answered. He pulled a towel off the rack and handed it to her.

'No. I am smiling, but I am not happy. I am crying!' Sweety howled.

She wrapped the towel around herself and stepped out. Lallan followed her, water dripping off of him.

Sweety was in the small square room. She sat on the floor. 'What happened?' Lallan came next to her and sat. 'I am crying Lallan, I am crying,' Sweety was in tears.

'Are you okay?' Lallan asked her.

'I ditched my father. I wanted to live life as I wished. I wanted to spread my wings.' She stretched her arms out.

'Sweety, are you sure we are safe here? I don't know about the person who has arranged this place for you. But you know, your father will be searching for us everywhere.'

For the first time, Lallan wanted to hug her. He did not hesitate. Sweety felt warm in his arms. 'I need to crash, Lallan,' she murmured, her eyes half closed.

She opened the cupboard in the room, pulled out a man's shirt and changed into it. 'How can you just wear someone's shirt?' Lallan asked, looking uncomfortable. She pulled out another shirt and threw it to him.

'So can you!' She smiled. They changed, dried themselves up and sat on the small sofa.

'Play the guitar. At least strum it to make me sleep,' Sweety said.

'I have never even touched a guitar in my life,' Lallan protested, but picked it up anyway.

'Just play with the strings,' Sweety said sleepily.

Lallan gave it a shot, his fingers clumsily stumbling over the strings.

Sweety fell asleep. It was a long-due nap, almost like hibernation.

Lallan looked at her beautiful face resting on his lap. He kept strumming the guitar till she was deep in sleep.

Lallan rested his head on the back of the sofa. Both rested like two drenched birds resting in the nest, warm and sweet. Lallan was in love with Sweety. Sweety was in love with herself. Love had brought them together from the badlands of Patna to the madlands of Mumbai.

There was absolute silence for a few moments.

It was killed by a sharp mobile ring tone.

Lallan was startled. Sweety was still asleep.

Lallan looked around to find the phone. It was neither his nor Sweety's. Carefully shifting Sweety's head, he got up. He followed the sound. He spotted it on the bedside table with a note saying, 'This is for you!'

He just stared at the screen.

It read 'Babu calling.'

45

Meetu was filing her nails. This used to be her favourite hobby. Filing nails and then choosing the nail paint from her vanity case. All beauty conscious women in small towns are proud owners of a vanity case.

She was sitting by the window in her room, the one that faced Lallan's house.

Lallan's house was quiet, but somehow seemed disturbed. She wanted to go and enquire about it, but stopped herself. She thought to herself that she had already stooped to her lowest in love and that was it. She was not interested in going down any further.

Meetu's thoughts were focused on her last memories of Lallan, of when he had snubbed her badly. She felt disturbed all of a sudden. She put down the filer and picked up the nail cutter instead.

Meetu cried as she cut her nails. She wanted to hate Lallan, forget Lallan and do away with him altogether, but he hovered in her mind.

Then, her mobile phone rang. She decided not to pick it up since the number looked like it was from some call centre.

Meetu got up, pulled open the drawer of her study table and pulled out her iPad. She went through the photos at random and started deleting every photo that had Lallan in it. There weren't many of those. Even if he had been present at the time, he was not in the photo. He looked the most uninterested of all the people in the frame in whatever photo happened to include him. Meetu couldn't spot a single picture that had Lallan smiling.

It was not easy to erase Lallan from her memories.

The phone still rang frantically. The number still appeared the same. Very close to the landline number of some call centre. Meetu was quite irritated by now. She picked up the call. 'Yes?' she asked in a stern voice.

'We are calling from Reliance Mobile network. We want to inform you that the service to your prepaid number will be barred permanently as the prepaid balance has been at zero for a long time now. You don't seem to use this phone number any more,' said a woman.

'I have a post-paid number, and my bill has been paid. You must be mistaken!' Meetu replied.

'No, madam, this number is in your name. Your date of birth is 10 March 1992?'

'Yes, that's right,' said Meetu.

'The number is 9343486872!' the voice on the other side said confidently.

'That number is definitely not mine,' Meetu frowned.

'This number has been active for three months now, ma'am.'

'Oh, okay. Ya, I think my brother uses this!' Meetu said to get done with the conversation. 'Can you send me the call records now, to my email address?'

'Sure ma'am, you need to send a request. I will be sending a message for e-billing. Please follow the steps and you will get the bill in few minutes.'

'Thank you so much.' Meetu cut the call. She quickly followed all the instructions and checked her inbox. She could just see one number on the call list.

Meetu called that number; it was switched off. She could sense something really fishy.

She put on her dupatta, tied her hair in a loose bun and rushed to her scooter. She had to get to the local Reliance office.

She needed to know everything.

46

Lallan was about to pick up the phone. Sweety rushed up and stopped him at the last moment.

'Wait! Don't pick up the phone now!'

'I am getting confused. What we are doing is not right. Who is helping us? I don't even know the person,' Lallan complained.

'It's all about trust! Nothing else!' Sweety said in a playful tone, trying to reassure him.

'I am a very simple person Sweety. I understand the world through Philip Kotler.'

Sweety threw her arms around him. 'Mr Kotler's nephew, let's do a SWOT analysis,' she grinned. 'You know about SWOT?' Lallan smiled. 'Strength, weakness, opportunity and threat,' giggled Sweety.

'Now tell me strengths of marrying someone like me!' she said.

'Marrying?'

'Yes. Marrying!'

'I have to answer?' Lallan raised an eyebrow.

'If you like me even a bit!' Sweety played with her hair.

'Okay. So, I will have a rich father-in-law!'

'That's it?!' Sweety moved away. She sat on the sofa with a grumpy face. This made her look much more beautiful than ever.

'I will be married to the most beautiful girl in the whole world with the sweetest name, Sweety Pandey!' Lallan joked.

'As if your name is Ranbir Kapoor! Look at you, Lallan Jha!' mocked Sweety. She looked grumpier now.

'Can I say the most honest thing? If I get married to you, I will get married to the most honest girl I have ever met. I see truth dancing in your eyes,' Lallan said, looking into her wide eyes.

Sweety looked down suddenly.

'What happened? Are you shy now?' Lallan tried to get her to look at him. Sweety could not meet Lallan's eyes.

'Am I wrong Sweety? Don't you have the most honest eyes?' asked Lallan. He wanted to kiss her now. Sweety resisted. 'We will have to inform Papa,' Sweety said, suddenly serious.

'He would be raving mad!' Lallan panicked.

'Listen. I know him. Just tell him that I sabotaged this plan for our safety. If he gets to know that we are safe, he will be fine,' she said.

'No. He must be really, really mad by now,' Lallan sounded sceptical.

'Who knows him better, you or me?' Sweety asked Lallan.

'We know him differently,' Lallan answered.

'We need to confess our love Lallan,' Sweety told him.

'Later.' Lallan looked away.

'It would be now or never. I know my dad. If he doesn't listen to us, we will run away!'

'That's just inviting danger to our doorstep.'

'You have come this far in love Lallan. We are now just a step away,' Sweety encouraged him.

'Sweety, do you know it will all appear fixed?' Lallan asked. Sweety was Kaali Pandey's daughter. She was not ready to give way on anything.

'What if we get killed?' asked Lallan.

'Do you want to live a life like this? You want to live like my father's slave all your life?'

Lallan had no answer.

'You have to make the relationship equal. You are not his slave. You will marry his only daughter.'

'He is very possessive about you!'

'And that is where you will win Lallan!' Sweety gazed into his eyes confidently.

Lallan hesitated.

'Don't think. Let's just get married. It will end everything. We faked this plan. Let's do it! Let's get money to my father and in return he could just get us married. That's not a bad deal!' Sweety was talking like an MBA graduate now.

Lallan thought it over for a bit.

'Let me call him from this mobile. Let's talk to him together,' Lallan went to pick up the phone in the bedroom.

'Stop!' Sweety shouted. 'You call him from a phone booth. This mobile thing will get us in trouble.'

'You come with me,' Lallan said.

'No. You go alone. I will pray here,' Sweety entreated.

Lallan melted, as always.

'Go, Lallan, tell my dad that you will marry me. Win me!' Sweety kissed Lallan on his forehead.

Lallan stepped out of the flat like a general off to conquer a city for his queen!

Sweety and Lallan looked at each other with an ocean of love for each other in their eyes. It was a very passionate moment. A very precious one. It was full of love and hope. The hope of love forever.

47

Kaali Pandey was sitting in a chair with his foot raised on a small stool and Ghonchu was giving him acupuncture.

Needles were pressed into his rough, large feet. 'Blood pressure feeling low?' asked Ghonchu.

'Till I get Sweety back,' Kaali said with a heavy heart.

Meetu was sitting opposite him. She had vengeance in her eyes and call records in her hand. 'What brings you here?' Kaali asked her.

'She is Lallan's neighbour,' said Ghonchu.

'I asked her, not you!'

'I was not just a neighbour to Lallan, I was his fiancée.' Meetu had tears in her eyes.

'So Lallan's father has sent you. Go and tell him this tactic will not work! If his son has outsmarted me in any way, I will kill him!' Kaali's nostrils flared in anger.

'What if your daughter betrayed you?' Meetu asked hesitantly.

'Get up and go!' Kaali shouted at her.

Meetu placed the call records in front of him. 'Lallan and Sweety were having an affair,' Meetu said fearlessly.

'Impossible!' Kaali didn't want to hear the truth.

'See for yourself. Lallan misused my ID card to get a prepaid mobile number in my name. He used to call only one number. That number is your daughter's, Sweety Pandey's.'

Kaali looked at Ghonchu. 'Did it start during the driving lessons?' Kaali asked him. Ghonchu shrugged.

'They deceived you all!' Meetu smiled with tears of vengeance in her eyes. Then she got up to leave.

Kaali Pandey was still trying to understand what had happened.

'I will take your leave,' Meetu said and walked out.

The mighty Minister Kaali Pandey looked beaten. 'Call Saumya home!' he ordered Ghonchu.

48

Saumya was there in a jiffy. It was only her and Kaali Pandey in the living room. It was almost like an emergency. Saumya was frightened almost out of her wits.

'You must know something?' Kaali Pandey asked her.

'No, uncle, like what?' Saumya lied.

'You're lying!'

'Uncle, you know how she is,' Saumya defended herself.

'She asked you to hide it. She wanted to run away with a loser like Lallan!' Kaali blasted her.

'She did not listen to me!' Tears welled up in Saumya's eyes.

'Shame on you! I wanted her to get married to your brother and you helped her in getting involved with a jerk—with a slave!'

'No, uncle. I always discouraged her. She smuggled him into my room once, during Satyanarayan Katha. I knew this girl would get us all into trouble one day,' Saumya started crying.

'I've been fooled! The world thinks my daughter has been kidnapped. If they get to know the real story, my whole political career will become a joke. I would never be able to face it!' Kaali Pandey said angrily.

'I have no clue about her. She didn't even tell me about this,' Saumya said helplessly.

'Where is she with the boy? I need them right here!' Kaali looked frustrated.

'You know what? Maybe Ghonchu knows more about it. He is not that simple! He was there during the blossoming of their love, during driving lessons,' Saumya hinted, trying her best to get herself off Kaali Pandey's list of suspects.

Kaali looked doubtful.

'Uncle, may I go?' pleaded Saumya.

'Don't tell this to anyone, not even to your family!' warned Kaali Pandey.

Saumya touched his feet and left quickly.

'Saumi!' called out Kaali.

She stopped.

'Do you really think it could be Ghonchu?'

'No. I don't know. I just thought . . .' Saumya fumbled.

'I don't trust my heart, but I trust Ghonchu,' said Kaali.

The mansion's dim chandelier cast shadows on Kaali Pandey's pale face.

49

Ishaq da kalam, junoon di siyaahi
Likhan baitha afsaana, chhap gayi tabaahi

Lallan read the beautiful love poem written on an autorickshaw parked near the mosque at Mandir-Masjid Marg.

Lallan felt like he was floating in air. Love was like a veil of bougainvillea swinging slowly with the wind. He knew that he was going to battle with the man he had grown up fearing.

Love can never belittle anyone's morale.

Lallan's self-esteem rose like the foam in a cup of espresso straight from the coffee machine. His throat was not dry like a desert for the first time ever. His eyes were not burdened by slavery, by always looking down. His face was not sweating.

Lallan soaked himself in his new-found state of love and belonging amidst the quaintness of this little lane on Yari Road.

50

Ghonchu started pressing the acupuncture needle firmly, so much so that Kaali Pandey screamed.

'Aiyee! Leave it!' Ghonchu's hand darted back.

'Should I get some tea sir, or some scotch?' Ghonchu asked his master.

Kaali Pandey took the glass vase kept beside and threw it at the chandelier, just as Sweety used to break the chandelier in anger. Ghonchu got scared.

'I will not even take a drop of water till I get my Sweety back and till I kill that bastard Lallan!' Kaali Pandey cried out. Then he cried like a baby. Ghonchu was afraid to even go near and comfort him. A monster was crying for his most precious love.

'This is how my Sweety used to vent out her anger on me. She used to break my expensive chandeliers. I have changed about twelve since she was born. I miss my Sweety, why did she do this to me?' he wailed.

'We will find her,' Ghonchu said in a faint voice.

'How?'

'Anyway we can.'

Kaali stretched his arms to embrace his most faithful subordinate. Ghonchu was dumbfounded; he had never seen his master like this.

'Come in to my arms,' Kaali sobbed. Ghonchu looked even more confused.

'Come,' Kaali invited him again, widening his arms as far as they could stretch. Ghonchu went up to him with slow steps. Kaali embraced him like a young boy hugging fresh candy floss right from the machine.

'You will never spill the truth, right?' asked Kaali.

'Never.'

'You will never tell Sweety the story of her mother, will you?'

'Not till the day I die.'

'Does she know something? Why did she take her mother's sari with her?' Kaali Pandey was suspicious. Ghonchu could sense it.

Kaali jerked Ghonchu away and held him by his throat.

'You know it right?' asked Kaali Pandey.

'Nothing. Trust me, sir,' said Ghonchu.

'You do.' Kaali Pandey tightened his grip.

'I have been with you since I was a kid. I have known everything, seen everything. I have only ever served you faithfully. I have been with you for thirty years. You don't trust me?' Ghonchu struggled to breathe.

'I will kill everyone. I don't trust anyone now. I have been cheated. Who has kidnapped Sweety? Where is she? If you are in on the plan, I will not spare you!' Kaali roared.

'I came to you when I was just seven years old. I was an orphan. I thought I had been blessed with a real god in my life who adopted me.' Ghonchu's eyes were popping out.

'You know about Sweety. Tell me.' Kaali didn't let go.

'You gave me shelter, a place to call home. Instead of giving me a toy, you gave me a gun.' A tear ran down Ghonchu's face.

'So you are blaming me for what you are?' Kaali Pandey glared at him.

'No one has ever dared to blame you for anything!' Ghonchu choked.

'Oh, yes! Now someone without any voice also has a voice.' Kaali Pandey's eyes were practically on fire.

'You killed the innocent childhood of Lallan too. Who knows, he might have actually taken his revenge!' Ghonchu's heart was coming out through his meek voice.

The meeker his voice became, the stronger his heart was getting.

'Oh, there is so much poison in your heart?' Kaali Pandey clenched his teeth.

'Good you tried to squeeze it out today by killing me! I served you loyally. I was more loyal than even a dog, in spite of you making me a Ghonchu from Dinesh Lal Mahto.'

Kaali Pandey suddenly came to his senses. He let go of Ghonchu's neck. Ghonchu looked like a goat just released from the butcher's hand.

'I am sorry. I don't know what came over me. I am losing my balance. I just want my Sweety back,' Kaali said.

Ghonchu got up, breathing heavily. He stepped back, looking at Kaali. His eyes were blank. His crooked body was like a frog leaping backwards.

Ghonchu took out his pistol. He had kept this pistol to guard his monster of a master.

'What are you doing? I told you I just got mad and lost all my control. You know me well.' Kaali was scared.

'You mistrusted me, your dog!' Ghonchu wept.

'You know how mad I am getting! You know my whole story; you know what happened to Sweety's mother! You know how much I love Sweety! I was just angry! I trust you Ghonchu, I trust you,' Kaali babbled.

'You have fear in your eyes. But look into my eyes. I am fearless. You know why?' Ghonchu asked, aiming the pistol at Kaali Pandey.

'Ghonchu. Don't react like a fool. It's not a toy gun beta, it's a real one.' Kaali tried to calm him down.

'I am fearless because I am a dog. I have never done wrong to my maalik, even though he was a monster.'

Kaali Pandey held his breath.

'So now, when my faithfulness has been doubted, my work as your slave is over. A dog is just about that!' Ghonchu stared at him.

'You gave this seven-year-old a toy called a gun. Now this thirty-seven-year-old wants to get away from this toy!' said Ghonchu quietly. 'Forgive me, Maalik, if I ever made you feel that I was a wrong horse you were betting on!'

By now, Kaali Pandey had lost all hope. He could see the face of Yama, the god of death, in Ghonchu's face. He could think just one thing and that was 'Goodbye.'

Ghonchu tensed. Kaali Pandey threw himself down with his eyes closed. Ghonchu fired.

Kaali looked up.

Ghonchu had shot himself in the head.

Blood was splattered all over Kaali Pandey and his living room. Kaali dragged Ghonchu's body to his Ambassador and stuffed him in the boot. He speeded his car towards Mahatma

Gandhi Setu connecting Patna and Hajipur. It was a pitch-dark night. He dumped Ghonchu's dead body in the Ganges. He dumped him where he had found him thirty years ago, at the Ganga Ghat, an orphaned boy with a hump.

51

Lallan had reached the phone booth near Mandir Masjid Marg.

'I need to make a call,' Lallan told the phone booth guy.

'Your accent says you are a bhaiyya from the north,' the booth owner said questioningly. Lallan was sweating heavily. Loudspeakers were all around and the Ganpati celebration had spun a coloured web in the city.

The booth owner offered some paan to Lallan.

'Where from? Bihar?' the man asked.

'No, not from Bihar. I'm from Delhi,' Lallan lied.

The booth owner took away the paan. 'Dilliwalas are fraudsters. I am a Bihari, we are known as bhaiyyas in Mumbai along with our UP counterparts and to eat my paan you have to be a bhaiyya.'

'Can I make my call?' asked Lallan.

'Keep the door open,' ordered the owner.

'Why?' Lallan looked amused.

'Ventilation,' the man smiled.

'I'll do just fine without ventilation.'

The man smiled and turned away.

Lallan dialled Kaali Pandey's number with fear. Kaali had a unique caller tone. It was a very high-octane song from Ram Gopal Verma's *Sarkaar* starring Amitabh Bachchan:

Saam daam dand bhed
Saam daam dand bhed
Govinda Govinda Govinda Govinda Govindaaaaa
Saam daam dand bhed
Govinda Govinda Govinda Govinda Govinda.

The tone always gave the caller an impression that a war was about to begin. In Lallan's scheme of things, whatever the type of war, it just had to be one-sided. Whatever was going to be the eventuality of this war, one thing was for sure—Lallan Jha's heart was going faster than the Olympic gold medallist at the hundred-metre sprint.

52

Kaali Pandey was sitting in a pool of blood. He could see his empire melting into the splattered blood.

Ghonchu had been like his spare tyre—the extra wheel without which the car feels incomplete. Suddenly, his phone rang, echoing throughout the mansion.

Kaali picked up the call, shaking off his morbid thoughts.

'Hello,' Lallan said, mustering all his courage.

'Where is my Sweety?' roared Kaali Pandey.

'Sweety is safe with me. We are in Mumbai. We had to change the plan because—' The words tumbled out of Lallan's mouth.

'I want her back!' Kaali Pandey demanded.

'We are working as per the plan; we will come back soon sir. We are hiding safely. You need not worry—'

'I demand my Sweety back!' screamed Kaali Pandey.

'Sir, we are in love, we want to get married,' Lallan muttered feebly.

'That girl was right!' Kaali gasped.

'Which girl?' asked Lallan.

'The one you were going to marry,' Kaali Pandey snapped.

'I never wanted to marry her,' Lallan retorted.

'You and Sweety fooled me with you plan. You used my situation!' Kaali was heartbroken.

'No, sir, I am not a fraud. I will bring Sweety back. Our plan will go as it is. I have just called to confess that Sweety and I love each other,' Lallan said.

'How dare you even suggest these things?'

'I want to seek permission. I am getting married to Sweety.' Lallan's voice grew stronger. He was unapologetic.

Kaali was quiet. He was still reeling from the shock of Ghonchu's suicide.

'I have always feared you for nothing. For a change, I want to put aside all my fear. I have not committed any crime. I love Sweety and my feelings are pure.'

'There's bloodshed in the near future, Lallan. Now no one will escape,' Kaali warned him.

'I just read a beautiful *shayari*. I wanted to recite it to you. I know, you have never heard a shayari, because you have not known what love is. Even I had never read shayari. I tried seeing the world through the eyes of Philip Kotler, and today was the first time a beautiful shayari stole my heart. It gave me strength to speak to you openly.'

'You know you will be killed,' Kaali said coldly.

There was silence at both ends.

Lallan smiled and disconnected the call. He wasn't scared of death any more.

53

Meetu was on her scooter, riding about aimlessly.

She did not want to go home. She had always found her shelter in Lallan. Her shelter was gone now. She knew that Lallan would never be hers.

Meetu's face was soaked with tears. She was on Fraser Road. She stopped at Basant Vihar, the famous dosa place, where Lallan had eaten paper dosa with her.

That was the only sweet memory of Lallan she had, where he'd taken care of her for a moment, even if it had been destroyed soon after.

Meetu parked her scooter outside.

She entered the restaurant. She saw the seat where she had sat with Lallan the other day. It was occupied.

'Madam, if you are alone, there is a seat vacant there,' the waiter said to her, pointing at a corner seat.

'No, I will wait for that one,' Meetu said.

'It will take another thirty minutes or so, madam!' the waiter said. He vaguely remembered seeing her before. 'Oh! You are the same madam! Sambar fell on you that day! You came with that gentleman who gave me a heavy tip! Is sir coming too? There is a good table for two.'

'Sir has run away with another girl. Now don't chew my brains. Just get me the table I want,' Meetu snubbed him.

The waiter retreated.

Thirty minutes later, Meetu was seated at the same table as the last time. Another waiter came to take her order.

'Order, madam?' he asked, grinning. He had already been cautioned by the other waiter.

'I want that dosa—the biggest one,' Meetu said.

'Sada paper dosa?'

Meetu had tears in her eyes. That was the only dosa Lallan used to eat. The last time too, he had been raving about it.

An old Mehdi Hassan ghazal was playing in the restaurant.

Mujhe tum nazar se gira to rahe ho,
Mujhe tum kabhi bhi bhoola na sakoge

Meetu could barely hold back her tears. When the heartbroken want to be brave, they eat. Eating or travelling diverts the mind. That's written in the rule book of the lost souls of love.

The sada paper dosa, shaped like a large boat, arrived. All the people at the nearby tables were looking at her.

Lallan's words came to her mind: 'It draws attention. Everyone looks at you.'

Meetu folded the dosa from both the ends like Lallan used to, and started eating it in small bites. Her eyes were full of tears.

54

Pegasus Apartments

Lallan came back to the apartment. His heart was racing. He felt like a lover who doesn't give a damn. He didn't take the lift. He wanted to feel the rush so he took the stairs and reached the flat. He pressed the bell. No one opened the door. He pressed the bell like a little boy who has come home thirsty after playing in the heat and wants to gulp a bottle of water straight from the fridge.

No one answered the doorbell. He started knocking the door. Again, there was no answer. Everything stood still for a moment. Lallan's heart skipped a bit. Why was Sweety not opening the door? Was she asleep?

He frantically rang the bell and knocked on the door.

Not a single sound came from inside.

Lallan looked at the row of flowerpots. He searched under each of them. He found a bundle of thousand-rupee note and a note under the fourth one. He opened it in hurry. It was a letter from Sweety.

```
Lallan,
    Forgive me!
    I had to contrive this plan to reach
my real love. There was no way out.
    I did not mean to use you, but there
was no way I could have reached Mumbai
alone, to my real love and my real dreams.
    Hope this money will help you sail
through.
    Sweety
```

Lallan was aghast.

He couldn't believe what he had got into. His head swam.

This was the biggest betrayal in his life. He had been used like a chopping board to cut the vegetables and had been thrown away with the peels.

He was also in the lion's trap. He was now Kaali Pandey's most hated enemy.

Kaali would never believe this story. He would think that Lallan had hidden Sweety. Lallan knew he would be eliminated. But more than getting the fear of being killed, he felt the pain of having his heart shattered.

He remembered how he had told Sweety that her biggest strength was her honesty. He could not believe that this whole journey had been contrived. Had she never loved him? Had she planned all this not to help him, but to come to Mumbai to run away with her lover?

Was she as cruel as her father?

Lallan had been punched straight on his heart. His mind went blank for a moment. Two seconds passed. Lallan could barely see anything.

He kept the money and the note in his pocket.

He tried to hold a railing or something; he couldn't find one, and he fell down with a thud.

Everything was going black.

Lallan lay there, unconscious, for a while.

The flats on that floor were vacant. The lift stopped there nonetheless, the person inside had accidentally pressed the wrong button. A burqa-clad woman with her son.

'Ammi! Someone is there,' the little kid pointed towards Lallan. The woman looked at him suspiciously. They walked towards him and realized he was unconscious as they got closer. The kid emptied his water bottle on Lallan's head.

Lallan opened his eyes. 'Go and call the guard,' the mother ordered.

Lallan was still in a daze. A few minutes passed with him still on the floor and the lady staring at him. The kid came with the guard.

'Who are you, sir? Are you are a visitor? I saw you going up.' The guard wanted to cover this up.

'Sweety,' Lallan spoke with a dry throat.

'Who's Sweety?' asked the guard.

'Sweety . . .' Lallan repeated faintly.

Three faces stooped over him—the woman in the burqa, the kid with his empty bottle and a guard with a flourishing moustache.

Lallan lay there, helpless.

55

It was a spacious three-bedroom flat in the posh Oberoi Spring, a famous apartment complex in Lokhandwala, home to a number of Bollywood celebrities.

Sweety was sitting with her guitar, a smile on her face. She was sitting across from a man with broad shoulders.

'See, I'd challenged you!' Sweety said.

The man was silent.

'You told me that our relationship would not work as I could never come to Mumbai physically. I did whatever it took—'

'You should not have run away from home!' the man said sternly.

'You don't care! Do you know how long it took to plan this out?' Sweety kept her guitar aside.

The man went and sat next to her. He put the TV on full volume.

He leaned in close and kissed her. Sweety smiled. He slid his hands under her shirt and unhooked her blue bra.

'We can do this later. You haven't even talked to me.' Sweety stopped him.

'You know you are irresistible,' he said, pulling her close. Sweety pushed him away.

'I am not an engine. I can't just get turned on and off like some machine. I am a girl, Sandy.'

'You are a dangerous cat, Sweety, not just some ordinary *chhuimui* girl,' Sandy mocked.

Sandy was a typical hunk. He was wearing a crisp, white shirt. He had his sunglasses on. His hair was wet and set with lemon-scented gel.

'Don't think that I am just another small-town girl!' warned Sweety.

'How could I, baba? I still can't forget the day when I saw the Britney Spears of Patna,' said Sandy.

'You might be a famous choreographer in Mumbai, but for me you are my Babu,' Sweety said. 'It was not easy Sandy. I have ditched my father, an innocent guy and my best friend to reach you. I wanted to break out of the cage. You always thought I could never do it,' Sweety said, putting her hands around his neck.

'What! You have secretly vanished from there. They would be looking for you. I arranged the flat for you somehow,' said Sandy.

'Actually, I have been kidnapped. The police are looking for me.'

'What are you saying now? Kidnapped?' Sandy was shocked.

'Don't be scared. You won't get caught up in all this,' Sweety assured him.

'You have gotten yourself kidnapped. They will be searching for you everywhere.' Sandy was getting scared.

'Relax. I will manage it,' Sweety assured him.

'You are a mad girl. I don't know what you are getting me into!' Sandy screamed in panic.

Sweety was crestfallen.

'Give me the flat keys,' Sandy said.

'By the way, whose flat was that?' asked Sweety.

'None of your business,' Sandy tried to change the topic.

'I want to rest. Can I sleep here?' Sweety spread herself on the sofa.

'Not even for a second.' Sandy pulled her up.

'Where will I go? Don't worry, they will not find you! No one knows about our affair. No one knows that we met in Patna where you came as a judge for Pop Diva and we fell in love.' Sweety tried to hold his hand.

'Now you are behaving like a small-town girl!' Sandy snubbed her.

'I had no way out, Sandy. My father would never let me out. I had to escape to Mumbai like this. I had to mislead a poor innocent guy called Lallan to reach you!' Sweety's eyes welled up.

Sandy looked furious.

'Wait. I have a friend's place. He lives alone. You will have to go and stay with him,' Sandy tried to get her to leave.

'Do you just want to get rid of me?'

'I'm only trying to hide you, baba. People know me, you will be seen and you can't live here with me,' he replied.

Sweety sat down with her face in her hands. She'd gone to him like a dreamy little girl rushing to her prince charming to complete the fairy tale.

'Come on, get up now,' Sandy stood impatiently.

Sweety got up and picked up her guitar and the sari.

'What's that?'

'My mom's sari. I will wear this when we get married,' Sweety looked at him with love.

'You are a crazy girl, Sweety!' Sandy said, searching for his car keys.

Sweety slid her hand in his back pocket and took out the keys. He hugged her.

'Come I need to make arrangements,' Sandy whispered.

'You love me, don't you, Babu?' Sweety asked, her voice full of emotion.

He hugged her again.

'I have got money in this bag.' She pointed at the little bag which was stained with pickles.

'Money?' Sandy was curious.

'I need to keep it safe,' Sweety was concerned.

'Don't worry. I will keep it safe, very safe,' he assured her.

Sweety stood in a corner, watching Sandy stack up the bag of money into his drawer. She held her mom's sari and her guitar tight.

56

Lallan Jha was having a heart-to-heart with the security guard. 'Should I talk to the society manager?' asked the guard.

Lallan gave him a five hundred–rupee note and told him not to get too excited.

'You are daydreaming, sir. This flat has always been shut. The owner is Mona madam, who lives in Dubai,' the guard told him.

'Maybe someone else has the keys,' Lallan argued.

'What's the girl's name?' asked the guard.

Lallan gave him another five hundred and whispered, 'Sweety.'

'The best thing would be that I should call up Mona madam directly on the phone and find out from her,' the guard said brightly.

'Yes, please do that.'

'Don't you have a bigger, red-coloured note? I am bored with green!'

Lallan took out a thousand-rupee note and handed it over.

The guard took out his phone and dialled a number.

'Your friend, madam, Sweety. Have you given her the keys to your flat?' the guard asked after explaining who he was and why he had called.

'Who is Sweety? I don't know any Sweety,' Mona said anxiously.

'No, nothing madam. It's just some confusion,' the guard reassured her.

'Okay. Everything is all right?'

'Yes, madam. I just wanted to ask for security reasons. You haven't given the keys to any friend or anyone in your family? A strict regulation will be passed soon by the committee.'

'No, no. Both the keys are with me,' said the lady.

'Okay, madam. Thank you.'

The guard looked at Lallan. 'Now either you have been dreaming or someone has tricked you big time!'

Lallan got up and left in a hurry, absent-mindedly thanking the guard for his help. At that moment, all he wanted to do was to get away from the place as soon as possible. He knew he had been tricked after all.

57

Minister Kaali Pandey had received three follow-up reminders from Radhey Shyam Yadav.

Kaali was unaware that his own pawn, Sudhanshu Yadav, had offered a vast amount of money to Radhey Shyam to leak the video. The media exposé would jeopardize Kaali Pandey's chances of winning the next assembly elections and leave Sudhanshu Yadav as the next potential candidate from the party. As Sudhanshu was also a Yadav, he wouldn't lose out on the caste's vote bank. His plan was well thought out.

Kaali Pandey was beginning to panic in any case. He hadn't been able to arrange the money Radhey Shyam Yadav had demanded to keep the video secret. To top it all off, he had lost his daughter Sweety and his closest henchman, Ghonchu.

He had called in a fleet of goons to instruct them to somehow get hold of Lallan and Sweety.

'The booth from which he called had been traced to Yari Road, Versova. He must be there. We will find them, sir,' said the leader of the goons.

'Just get my daughter back safely, kill the guy if need be. Just get my daughter!' Kaali shouted, feeling helpless.

Just then, Kaali got a call. It was Saumya.

'Uncle, I have to tell you something.'

'Did you hear anything about Sweety?'

'She had a friend in Mumbai, maybe he would help us. He is a choreographer. He had come here as judge for that Patna Pop Diva Contest,' Saumya reminded him.

'You have his number?' asked Kaali.

'I will try to get it; maybe I can contact him on Facebook. Maybe she has already gotten in touch with him,' said Saumya.

'Do that, beta. Get my Sweety back!' begged Kaali.

'Sure, Uncle. I will do everything I can. I will call you back as soon as I hear from him,' Saumya tried to calm him down.

Kaali Pandey sat on his royal sofa, sweat beading his forehead. He looked at the broken chandelier and sighed.

58

Sandy stopped the car. It was dark. 'Come out,' he said. Sweety got out of the car with her guitar half-heartedly. She stared at the dilapidated old building.

'Don't worry, it's Mumbai. Most of the buildings here are like that. These buildings are like coconut, hard, rough and ugly from the outside, but quite nice from within,' Sandy tried to convince her.

'Where are you putting me up?' asked Sweety.

'Not at any stranger's place, baby. It's my old aunt,' said Sandy. He had a key. He opened the creaky door on the ground floor. A cat jumped out. 'Jhoothi,' he said, petting the cat.

Sweety got scared. 'Jhoothi?'

'Yes, that's what my aunt calls her cat,' Sandy tried to make it sound normal. He walked inside. The drawing room was in a mess. Empty medicine packets and cat food were littered all over the place. He switched on the lights.

'Don't dump my ashes in Mehboob Studio. I have changed my mind,' a heavy voice came from inside another room.

'I have not come to collect your ashes. I have come with a friend.' Sandy walked inside.

Sweety followed. The sight of Sandy's aunt terrified her. She looked dangerous in a checked nightie, her hair uncombed and tangled.

'Don't worry, this is just my rehab look,' the lady started laughing.

Sweety laughed along feebly, trying to hide her uneasiness.

'Sweety will live here for some time, Buaji,' Sandy explained.

'Oh. Then tell her that I don't want my ashes to be thrown in Mehboob Studio. I prefer Kamalistan. It has better space, less pollution.' The old lady went into the kitchen. The cat went behind her.

'Don't panic. Relax. Sit. It's the safest place,' Sandy tried to make Sweety comfortable.

'What is this Mehboob Studio? What is Kamalistan? What did she say?' Sweety looked puzzled.

'She is like a puzzle. You can be with her forever and keep trying to solve it,' Sandy smiled.

'Sandy. What are you doing? I have come to be with you. I can't live here! What is she saying? I don't understand.' Sweety began to pace.

'She's just an old, depressed, struggling actress! She won't hurt you. The cat is less dangerous than you, by the way,' Sandy shouted.

'Don't shout at me!'

'You will get me in trouble! You said you are coming to meet me, but then you reveal this kidnapping story!'

'You are a headless a*****e,' Sweety screamed back at him with tears in her eyes.

He hugged her. 'Sweety, we have to be safe. You just stay here!' he cajoled her.

'You told me to leave everything and just come with my guitar. You said that we will realize our dreams together!'

'Yeah, I did say all of that. I did promise that. But you've gone ahead and done some crazy stuff! You have created a mess back home, and you have put me in danger too!' Sandy tried to push her away.

'Okay, so how long do I have to hide?' Sweety asked, as if she was prepared to be brave and put up in this strange house with a crazy old aunt.

'Until I fix up something. I will come to meet you every day!' Sandy promised her. He kissed her on her forehead and left.

The cat purred the whole night. The aunt slept with her Geeta Dutt music on.

Sweety was sitting up in bed, the table lamp on next to her. She sat awake the whole night contemplating what she had done. She spent the night thinking about her Philip Kotler, the serial entrepreneur, the Ambani in the making, Lallan Jha from Patna.

How she'd rested her head on his lap and how he'd strummed the guitar! Lallan was like a comforting pillow. She felt choked. She missed him.

No, she said to herself. Lallan had been just a means to an end—a route to the destination that was Sandy.

But then, she thought, the route of her journey had been much warmer and much more interesting than the cold destination.

What did she exactly want? The journey or the destination?

59

Sandy was driving. Love Guru was playing on the radio.

'Love guru, I think I love a girl. I masturbate for her. Is it love?' asked a listener.

Sandy frowned in disgust and switched to a station playing a fast-paced Bollywood song. He sighed with relief, as if he had just unloaded a heavy burden from his shoulders. He stopped the car at the Seasons Wine Shop. He got down and bought a chilled beer. He chugged it down quickly before going back to his car. He looked exhausted.

His phone pinged. He had a message on Facebook. It was from Saumya Gupta.

'Hi, I am Saumya, a friend of Sweety. She has been missing for a while now. We got to know that she is in Mumbai. Has she contacted you by any chance?'

Sandy wanted to ignore it but then something struck him and he chose to reply. 'Sweety? I don't know. Are you talking about the girl from Patna? No, I have no clue. She is missing?'

Sandy knew he was in deep trouble. Sweety was a trouble bubble that had suddenly landed into his life.

Sandy called up his friend Mitesh Patel on mobile.

'Patel, I need your help!' Sandy said urgently.

'Yes, bhai,' Patel spoke in his over-accented Gujarati.

'Come to the Mith Chowki signal. I need to speak to you.'

'Bhai, I am in bathtub.'

'It's just a bathtub. You are not on Jupiter,' Sandy said irritably.

'Okay Sandy bhai, I'm coming. Mith Chowki will be too far. Come to Jogeshwari signal.'

After some time, Sandy's car stopped at the Jogeshwari signal. Patel was waiting in a shirt that clung to his pot belly, with knee-length shorts. Patel waved. Sandy opened the door for him. He got in.

'What bhai? What's the matter?' asked Patel.

'Sweety.'

'Oh, your WhatsApp friend? Patna ki Shakira?' joked Patel.

Patel was a part-time real estate agent and a full-time producer.

'Not Shakira, Britney Spears.'

'Haan, haan, Britney Spears or Madonna,' joked Patel.

'She told me that she is coming to meet me, be with me for some time,' Sandy muttered.

'So, enjoy! You are a babe magnet, Sandy bhai!' Patel patted him on the shoulder.

Sandy looked worried.

'You need a flat for merry time?' Patel laughed. He took out a set of keys. 'Take this, my home free for you!' Patel assured Sandy.

'No, I don't need a room; I need to fix up something. This girl has put me in soup—a hot soup,' Sandy stopped the car.

He looked as if he had been put into a cage with a hungry tigress.

'Tell me the full story.'

60

Lallan was homeless. His scarred heart was not even racing. He was in a taxi with a muffler around the lower half of his face. The taxi was on Worli Sea Link. It was pitch-dark.

Lallan looked out at the sea and remembered the words of the taxi driver. He had shown them the spot where most people committed suicide. Lallan wanted to commit suicide.

He asked the taxi to stop.

'We aren't allowed to,' the driver said.

'No, it's urgent. Just drop me here and go,' ordered Lallan. His order was also like a request.

'As you say, but please don't commit suicide.' The taxi driver left after collecting his fare.

Lallan went to the corner of the bridge. The sea waves had always looked inviting on the shore, but now looked dangerous in the middle of the sea.

Lallan had wanted to be as rich and famous as Ambani one day. He wanted to rule the world. He wanted to shine with his business acumen one day. But that day had never come. His dream of a kidnapping insurance business had been manipulated by a monster's daughter.

Sweety had used him. Sweety had abused him.

Lallan still thought of Sweety's betrayal as something vaguely unreal, as it hadn't sunk in completely yet.

There was no point living like this. He decided he should jump and end his bloody life. He looked back and figured his life had been cursed early on, ruined in his childhood by Kaali Pandey and wrecked further by Kaali's daughter now.

One, two and three . . .

He was about to jump when a police constable stopped him, holding him by his shirt.

'Aye, thamba! You people don't even let us rest on Sunday!' the policeman scolded him.

Lallan was speechless.

'Who are you?' The constable stared at him. Lallan didn't say a word. Another policeman came running.

'What man? Suicide attempt? No job, love problem, what is it?' the second man asked.

Lallan still silent.

'Let's take him to the lock-up then!' announced the first policeman.

'It looks as if he hasn't eaten anything in a while.' The second policeman was softer at heart. He gave Lallan a fifty-rupee note.

'Go eat a vada pav. Have a cutting chai and think about life. Do not waste it like this. You are a young man, who knows, you may become an Ambani one day!' the policeman said, patting Lallan.

Lallan had tears in his eyes.

He saw Antilla shining in the distance. He knew his tall dreams had been erased forever now.

'Go, go. Let our Sunday be easy,' the other policeman said and smiled at him.

Lallan looked at the policemen. They looked like angels.

61

The night passed by.

Sweety realized that Sandy's Bua too had not slept the whole night. The Geeta Dutt music was still playing. Sweety went to the kitchen to make some tea. The fridge was stacked with beer bottles.

'I drink beer every morning,' said Bua.

Sweety turned around to see Bua right behind her.

'You didn't sleep?' asked Bua.

'You didn't sleep too,' said a scared Sweety.

'You are an invader. I don't sleep when an invader is in my home,' Bua told her sternly.

'I didn't want to stay here. Sandy has just . . .' Sweety looked helpless. She walked out of the kitchen and sat on the cot outside.

'This place smells! How can any living being stay here?' Sweety wondered out loud.

'Then why don't you become dead body like me?' Bua came running from the kitchen.

'I think you need rest,' said Sweety. She wanted to avoid talking to her.

Bua looked at her sternly.

'I need to go buy some bread.' Sweety went up to the door.

'The door is locked from the outside,' said Bua.

Sweety was shocked. What was the home equation? Why had Sandy dumped her here? What will she do now? She had ditched her father and Lallan to reach Sandy, but Sandy hadn't even looked at her! What did his behaviour mean? What did he intend to do?'

'Open the drawer. It has some packets of Bourbon biscuits. I love them. You can eat some of them,' said Bua and went inside.

Sweety opened the drawer and found the packet of Bourbon biscuits. It was open and soggy. She ate it. She knew by now that she has been living in an illusion. She had trusted the dream bubble of love. She was suffocated here. Stuffed, stifled and suffocated.

Sweety was still stuck in a cage—she had simply moved from one prison to another. This was perhaps the worst. She had at least been a princess in her father Minister Kaali Pandey's cage.

62

Pegasus Apartments was being raided by Kaali Pandey's goons. They reached the booth on Yari Road from where they had somehow traced their target address in Pegasus.

The guard was cross-questioned and the residents were grilled. The goons could sense that Lallan and Sweety had been there.

The tallest goon was Loha Singh. He could extract teeth out of a lion's mouth. The lot could finally make the security guard spill the truth.

The house belonged to Mona, who lived in Dubai. She had no clue that her keys had been duplicated. The guard used to rent it out to Patel who would rent it out to lovers.

'Give us Patel's number or we take you to Patna!' warned Loha Singh.

'Leave it, please!' The guard tried to be friendly.

Loha Singh held him by his neck.

'Sorry, sorry! I will tell you. I will give you his number. Spare me,' pleaded the guard.

After getting Patel's phone number, Loha Singh instructed his men to move from there.

'Bhaiyya . . . can I have some change if you don't mind?' The guard stopped them.

Loha Singh turned and slapped the guard and left with his cavalcade.

It was the fifth day of Ganpati Visarjan. There was chaos all over. Drums and loudspeakers had taken over the sound graph of the city.

Loha Singh and others had a tough task ahead—to find Lallan and Sweety within this chaos.

63

Lallan was sitting in a local from Borivali to Parel.

This was the best place to hide, from one local to another.

The insides of the train smelt of gajras, powder and sweat. The Ganpati Visarjan crowd squeezed him like a half-cut lemon. He was drenched in his own sweat.

Lallan knew that, by now, the hunt must be on. He had nowhere to go, nowhere to hide. How long could he spend in the local trains? The police would also be involved sooner or later. He had even escaped a suicide. He had spent the whole night rallying in different trains, repenting his life and love.

It was two at night and the local had stopped too. He had no place to go. The platform was not a safe place. Anyone could be easily spotted there. He sat quietly and alone.

He could not get Sweety out of his mind. The taxiwala who'd left them midway unconsciously came to his mind again and again.

He had told them a magical thing about the Haji Ali Dargah where a lot of people would come with their last hope. Lallan had nothing, just a hope! He knew that he still 'hoped'. He had lived in hope all his life for a happy tomorrow. The happy tomorrow never came. Still the hope flickered!

64

Dogs were barking outside. The cat was purring near Sweety's feet. Sweety knew dogs well but cats were strange to her.

But Bua looked stranger than the cat. She had had severe bouts of depression since morning. At times, she became Meena Kumari and talked about how Kamal Amrohi had made her life hell. On some other occasion she became Madhubala and cursed Kishore Kumar for not taking care of her when she was ill.

Sweety opened the biscuit drawer. She saw pictures taken during Bua's youth. She was a junior artist of yesteryears.

Sweety understood that she must have gone through a crisis. Someone held Sweety's neck from the back. It was Bua.

She started scratching and hitting Sweety badly.

'What are you doing?' Sweety screamed.

'You opened my book? Huh? How dare you?' Bua attacked Sweety with a photo frame.

Sweety tried to push her back. She was actually a weak woman. She fell down. The cat jumped on Bua, who started sobbing hard.

Sweety extended her hand to help her get up. She became aggressive again and held Sweety's neck. Sweety somehow dragged her to her room and locked her in. Bua kept banging the door. Sweety was scared as hell.

There was an old mad woman banging the door, a growling cat called Jhoothi and a scared Sweety. She could only see a window which was netted. She ran to the kitchen, got a knife and a pair of scissors. Somehow she tried to cut a hole in the net and jump out of the window. She left her guitar. She only took her mom's sari as a scarf.

Sweet had bruises and scratches on her body. She had no clue about what to do. She took an auto and reached Oberoi Springs, the plush pad of Sandy.

When she reached there, a guard stopped her.

'Madam?' asked the security guard looking at her state.

'Sandy . . . B 1105,' Sweety told the guard in hurry.

The guard called the house on the intercom. He informed Sweety that there was no one at home.

'No, you just spoke to someone, didn't you?' Sweety enquired.

'Madam, I am on my duty. You can't go inside. '

It was an electronic gate. Sweety had nowhere to go. She sat outside the building, all through the night, and shivered. She knew that she had been fooled in love.

Early in the morning a car stopped in front of her. It was Patel. He looked at Sweety.

'You are Sweety?' asked Patel. She nodded.

'Get in the car . . . I am Sandy's friend.'

Sweety looked apprehensive.

'Pegasus apartment . . . that's my apartment,' said Patel.

Sweety understood that they were connected. She sat in the car.

'You silly woman, you have put all of us in great trouble!' said Patel.

Sweety was in tears.

'Now your father's men have traced me also. They are looking for me. They got to know I helped you!' Patel blasted her.

'I want to meet Sandy,' pleaded Sweety.

'He has a name here. He has a life. Don't destroy it. Just go away!' Patel ordered.

'I will. I just want to meet him once,' pleaded Sweety.

'He is on a shoot. If I take you there, he will be in trouble,' said Patel.

'I will meet him in private for a few minutes. After that, I promise I will call my father, tell him the truth and go back,' Sweety said.

'Okay. Then let's go meet him one last time,' Patel said.

'I need to go to the parlour!' Sweety said, looking at Patel.

Patel was actually amused to see a girl like this. The parlour? Now?

'Please. My last wish!' pleaded Sweety, wiping her tears and trauma.

Patel gave up and took her to Enrich salon, in Andheri, amused all the while. This was Sweety who wanted to visit a parlour post trauma.

65

Sweety came out from the parlour, almost dry-cleaned and polished. She was changed. She looked like a diva. Exactly how Sandy had seen her for the first time, when he had come to hold an audition in Patna.

It had been love at first sight for Sweety. He had promised her a beautiful life in Mumbai. He had come back, but Sweety was still in her father's prison. Sandy looked like the only window to Sweety's life and aspirations. Her only agenda was to come running to him and get married to him. But yes, she was living in a love bubble. Sandy was avoiding her. Sweety could take anything but she could not take anyone ignoring her.

There was another issue—Lallan. She had intended to use him. But she could not deny that she had had a moment of truth with Lallan. Lallan made her feel warm—warm in the same way as she felt in her mother's sari.

But, for now, after getting a makeover, Sweety dressed herself in new clothes bought from a Westside store.

Patel waited all this while. He really could not figure out what this girl was all about. There was a smile on her magenta-coloured lips.

66

112th day

Loha Singh and gang could not trace Sweety and Lallan in the Ganpati festival mayhem. The infamous Minister Kaali Pandey could not get Sweety back. The deadline had arrived. The meeting was fixed in the same farmhouse.

Radhey Shyam and Kaali Pandey were face–to–face. It was a game of chess again. Radhey Shyam laughed hard, looking at a dishevelled Kaali Pandey, who stared at his dusty shoes.

'Have all your servants left you? No one left to clean your shoes?' Radhey Shyam was touching the wrong chords.

Kaali tried not to utter a single word.

'You look incomplete without Ghonchu,' Radhey Shyam tried his funny bone.

Kaali Pandey still didn't say a word.

'Heard your daughter has run away?' Radhey Shyam smiled his usual evil smile.

'She has been kidnapped,' Kaali said sternly.

'You could have gotten her married to my son. We might be from a lower caste, but we are of higher standard than of a slave.'

'My daughter will come back.' Kaali Pandey tried to look confident.

'Today's my deadline. Have you got the money?' asked Radhey Shyam.

'Yes,' said Kaali.

'I am surprised you managed it. You have a lot inside your *gaddi*. People underestimate you!' Radhey Shyam mocked.

'I want you to break the videotape. And I want assurance that you don't have a copy,' Kaali Pandey negotiated.

'I will. Trust me. I am more trustworthy than Ghonchu,' mocked Radhey Shyam.

'I don't mean to hold a conversation with a third-class man,' said Kaali Pandey.

'Third class is your offspring who ran away with a driver. Shame on you! Your wife committed suicide and your daughter ran away with a third-class man. No one wants to be with you.' Radhey Shyam Yadav tried to demean and humiliate Kaali Pandey.

Kaali Pandey pushed his suitcase forward.

'Your chela, your trusted successor Sudhanshu Yadav, offered me double to double-cross you!' said Radhey Shyam. 'I could have made the video viral and earned double. You would have been suspended and Sudhanshu Yadav would have contested the election. Simple game. But I want to play difficult games, Kaali Pandey,' Radhey Shyam could not control his boasts today.

'Open the suitcase only when you break the video in pieces.'

'You watch lot of Hindi films Pandeyji! The world has changed. It's the digital age. Breaking the record is only for old films.'

'I don't trust you!' said Kaali Pandey.

'Behead me if I go wrong. You are capable!' Radhey Shyam was fearless.

Kaali opened the suitcase. It had a pistol. Kaali took the pistol out and pointed at Radhey Shyam.

'Yes, I watch a lot of films. Pistols have still not become digital!' Kaali Pandey looked at him angrily.

'You can kill me. I have already instructed my people. You will also be dead. Your video will go viral. You were responsible for killing your young brother–in–law to gain public sympathy and win the election. Your daughter will learn the truth behind her mother's suicide and hate you more. She will never return to you!' Radhey Shyam warned him.

'I knew it would come back. My wife used to tell me that it would come back. I used to laugh it away, but now I realize she was right. My time has come, but I will win this last game of chess.' Kaali looked straight in his eyes.

'Put the pistol away,' said Radhey Shyam. His eyes were red.

'I will always remain the king, always!' Kaali Pandey aimed his gun at Radhey Shyam's chest.

Radhey Shyam was scared.

'You have hurt me right in my heart, now I will hurt you back there,' and, saying that, Kaali pulled the trigger.

The bullet hit Radhey Shyam's heart. He was dead in a matter of minutes.

67

Vanity van, Filmistan Studio

'Babu . . . I want to devour you,' she said.

This was Sweety. Her lips were painted magenta-red. She had a thing for magentas. It was that dangerous bloody thing between dark pink and dark red.

Sweety was actually going through an intermediary state of life. But for the moment, she wanted to deface his chest.

She held him in her slim sandalwood-infused arms. Her arms reeked of the Mysore Sandal soap she used daily to keep the aroma alive. He loved that smell, but today it was suffocating him. He wanted to push her away, even as she reached out to unbutton his shirt.

'Are you afraid or what?' She eyed him suspiciously.

'Come on.' He gathered himself and tried to kiss her on her eyes.

She did not want such sweet innocent shots of love. She was ready for a torrential downpour of raging hormonal romance.

'Let me kiss you all over on your chest. Let the world know . . . Babu is *my* property,' Sweety said breathlessly as she clasped his wrists and tried to unbutton his shirt.

He lightly shoved her, straddled her and unzipped his trousers. His boxers were pristine-white with a red jockey band.

'Your underwear has changed . . . *You* have bloody changed. Babu, you hiding something from me, aren't you?' Sweety let out a muffled protest.

He gagged her with his thick parched lips. They were cold like dried wax. He interlocked his sweaty palms with hers. She could sense the tension in every drop of the sweat coming off his palms.

It was time to take matters into her hands, literally!

She had him on his back, as she pushed against him like a tidal wave. Sweety was now on top.

The flashy light from the bulbs bordering the huge mirror of the vanity van fell straight on his face. His skin had sheen, quite like the moonlight. Sweety kissed him all over his face, bent down over his neck and got down to unbuttoning his shirt. He held her hands off like a cuff.

'Why won't you let me unbutton your shirt? You are behaving very strangely, Babu, what has happened to you?' Sweety was sure that something was up.

Sweety's hand held his shirt and was desperately trying to unbutton him.

'Just a sprain. I was at the gym . . . uh . . .' He uttered some lame words.

'You know what . . . when you look right . . . you are lying,' Sweety attacked him straight.

'You know what! You over-read. Don't look at me like that. I just had a sprain . . . That's it.' He tried to push her away.

'I can't make love to my Babu? Do I need permissions now?' Sweety asked petulantly.

She was overtly sexy. Her sex appeal was attached even to her pretty little chin; it was that soft conical chin, which became sexier as she pouted to show that she was upset.

'Come on, love me . . . pull off my jeans,' he said. Whether it was a request or an authoritative instruction, he wasn't sure. In fact, he was not sure about anything at that moment.

Sweety kept staring at him.

'Go down,' he whispered. 'Pull off my jeans, Sweety.' His voice trembled.

Sweety looked deep into his eyes. His eyes were light brown. In the guide book of coital flirting, dating a guy with light-brown eyes is the riskiest! Sweety did everything that was 'risky' for sure!

She scrambled down. He eased a little. He let go of her wrists. He adjusted his head on the little cushion of the vanity van. He knew that Sweety was about to give him waves of pleasure. Sweety unzipped him. He simply surrendered. Like a predatory cheetah, Sweety changed her course. In a matter of seconds, she tore his shirt. She knew something lay hidden beneath that shirt.

She was shocked. And speechless.

He was hiding something for sure.

There was a tattoo on his chest. It was the name of a girl. And it wasn't Sweety. It was 'Anu'.

The tattoo looked fresh. The skin around it was still red.

There was another woman in his life. Sweety could sense that she had been taken for a ride.

She punched his nose. A punch on the nose can shake your whole body—it is bloody hurtful. She left him wounded and bleeding. He owed her an explanation but she was not in a state to listen to one.

'Sweety—' he tried explaining but she was beyond it.

Sweety was high-strung by nature and would swing between extremes. She felt extreme love for him. Or may be extreme hatred for him—both emotions tearing through her at that very moment. There were no in-betweens here.

Some young girls and boys standing outside the vanity van could sense that some steamy lovemaking was definitely underway inside the mood-lit and cosy vanity van. The door of the van suddenly opened with a bang. All the heads turned towards the door. They saw a man's shoe being flung like a missile and then another. Nobody could miss the vanity bag that came flying next. All the crew members waiting outside were witness to the most dramatic scene that was not even part of the shoot.

Sweety walked out of the vanity van with her magenta lipstick smudged around her lips. She stormed out as if she was playing her part in an epic war saga. Nobody knew her on the set, at least none of the people standing around the vanity van. Her walk was super confident, reminding them of Chulbul Pandey from *Dabangg*. This filmy swagger was all but a ruse to keep people guessing whether she was a heartbroken girl or simply a catty bitch who broke the noses of handsome men. It was not easy to get to know the bundle of contradictions that Sweety Pandey was.

Two different worlds had been shaken, right to their core!

68

There was an eerie silence in Kaali's mansion. His mighty empire was plagued by misfortune. He stood staring at a huge painting of his dead wife hanging on the wall. There was another frame with a childhood photograph of Sweety.

Radhey Shyam's last words still resounded in Kaali's ears. And they were so true. Kaali's wife had committed suicide after she discovered his brutality. His daughter had eloped, leaving him humiliated. He had killed all his trusted followers. What was a king without his people?

In his desperation to win, Kaali had actually lost his own self. He was the biggest loser.

Kaali Pandey moved towards his table and pulled open a drawer, and stared at the fountain pen and the notepad lying inside it.

69

Sweety did not have the strength to go back and face her father. She knew that Lallan would never forgive her. But, deep inside, she wanted to apologize to both her father and Lallan.

The *ishqiyapa* had turned around on her. The one she loved had someone else in his life. Sweety had mistaken his false promises and flirting for love.

She actually never realized what love was until she was faking it with Lallan. The driving lessons, smuggling Lallan into Saumya's room, hiding in the truck, strumming the guitar and putting her to sleep—that was love.

Sweety knew that she had lost it. She wanted to take a train back to Patna, but before that she wanted to visit Haji Ali to get the strength to face the mess.

It was a high-tide day when Sweety reached Haji Ali. Lallan was also there, sitting in a corner path. Announcement of high tides were on. Lallan moved to other corner to save himself from getting wet. He walked with his little hope. He saw a mirage walking towards him. Was it Sweety?

Lallan hid himself in a corner. He saw a girl walk past him. Yes, she had the same sandalwood smell—Sweety's sandalwood smell.

'Sweety,' whispered Lallan. Sweety turned to see Lallan. Sweety ran to hug him but he pushed her away.

'You never loved me,' Lallan was in tears too.

'Punish me for what I did. God has already punished me, making me realize that my heart beats only for Lallan!'

'How do I trust you?' asked Lallan

'Come with me. We will go to Patna together, face my father and get married.' Sweety had her plan in place.

'It's childish. He will kill me.' Lallan knew Kaali's wrath.

'Let's die together then.' Sweety extended her arms.

A huge wave hit them and they had to hug each other.

It was true. Flickering hope gets a place in Haji Ali. Sweety and Lallan were together. Love got a new name!

70

Sweety and Lallan stood in front of Kaali's mansion on a sunny morning. There were no servants around. There was no Ghonchu. It looked abandoned.

Sweety and Lallan went inside and looked everywhere. There was no one. Sweety and Lallan walked to Kaali Pandey's bedroom. It was empty. She opened the door of her room. She found an envelope on the bed. She took out a letter.

I know you, Sweety. You will come back!
    I know you!
    You hated me outrightly, but loved me too.
    I lived all my life with an ego, a false pride and power.

A secret I had kept wrapped after
your mother's suicide is kept inside
your cupboard's drawer.

I know you will hate me more. I
deserve to be hated.

I had an option of killing myself.

I had another option of just vanishing.
I want to destroy myself and rebuild.

I don't know. I am going away. Far
away. Haven't decided where but, for
sure, somewhere where no one will ever
find me.

I will come back, beta, when I find
myself.

I am glad you found your love!

Blessings,

Kaali

Sweety stared at the letter for a long, long time. Lallan
stood by, holding her by her shoulders.

Kaali's mansion was no longer a prison. It was an open
cage which was on its way to becoming a nest—Sweety and
Lallan's nest.

What had started out as a hide-and-seek game of many
ishqiyapas and cross-connections turned into a true bond of
love and sacrifice. This was the ishq the poets talked about—
with the *siyapa*s being thrown out with the rubbish and the
all the garishness. It was time for some honesty and simplicity.
It was time to close the main door and check where all the
money and guns were, for, in Patna, you never know!

ACKNOWLEDGEMENTS

Happy people are thankful and thankful people are happy. So 'Thank You' becomes the shortest yet most effective ego massager in the world of formalities.

Let me take you to the world of Thank You Politics.

There are three types of Thank Yous:

1. **Moral Obligation:** This is a thank you at 'gun point'. This is for the person you are most scared of. So, this goes to my wife! I love her because I need her and I need her because I love her. This is a small thanks to our Love–Need equation which has kept me motivated to write about love, even after ten years of marriage. People who have been married for ten years otherwise write about salvation!

2. **Social Obligation:** This is a thank you at 'son point'. So, this is for my angry mother who has been upset because

I dedicated my previous novel, *What a Loser!*, to my mother-in-law! A son is like a see-saw between his own family and in-laws. So, this one is for my mother, to wash away her frowns and cribs.

3. **Financial Obligation:** This is a thank you at '*dhan point*'. Nothing seems funny without money. So to keep your smile going, you need smiley amounts in your bank account! Biggest thanks to my editor, Vaishali Mathur, who crafted a commercial-fiction author out of me! Thanks to her conviction and belief in me. Her encouragement and efforts have helped me to progress as a writer. I hope to be a rich, in fact, a very rich writer, soon.

What a Loser!
Pankaj Dubey

Of dreams and their consequences!

Pandey Anil Kumar Sinha (PAKS) comes to Delhi with precisely three things: one, his jaded old trunk full of sattu and achaar; two, a borrowed dream of becoming an IAS officer from his clerk father; and three, to sleep with a milky-white Punjabi girl.

However, PAKS's goals begin to change when he falls in love, enrols for English classes and finds cool friends. Then suddenly he is pushed to the forefront of university elections and he becomes a hero!

PAKS is living his ultimate dream . . . or is he?

What will happen next? Will he ever get what he really wants? Find out in this laughathon full of clichés straight from the cow belt of India!

My Fiancée, Me & #Ifu**edup
Aarya Babbar

'An unputdownable laugh riot'—Riteish Deshmukh

Rushabh Shah, 26, simple-hearted gujurati guy who's done nothing extraordinary in his life besides loving his girlfriend Mahek Chopra with complete loyalty n sincerity!

He has only 1 problem: he's confused about everythin! Still he manages taking the 1st decision of his life & proposes marriage to Mahek, who happily says YES!

The families r happy, the couple r more than happy but that's when—

The madness begins!

3 weeks left for his marriage . . .

15 yrs of love at risk . . .

Rushabh's gonna f**k up everythin!

How?

The answer lies in the book u hold.

Warning: This is not a #lovestory this is a #fu**upstory.